D0952161

The Wild Winter

WITCHES AT WAR III: The Wild Winter

First published in 2012 by
Pavilion Children's Books
10 Southcombe Street
London
W14 0RA

An imprint of Anova Books Company Ltd

ISBN 9781843651802

A CIP catalogue record for this book is available
from the British Library.

10 9 8 7 6 5 4 3 2 1

Printed and bound by 1010 Printing International Ltd, China

This book can be ordered direct from the publisher at the website:
www.anovabooks.com
or try your local bookshop.

WITCHES AT WAR!

The Wild Winter

MARTIN HOWARD

PAVILION
CHILDREN'S

Contents

Prologue

Blown from who-knows-where, a newspaper fluttered and whirled through the blizzard, its headline screaming "COLDEST WINTER *EVER!*" A gale howled, driving snow into the shapes of giants that toppled trees as they stomped across the landscape. Hour after hour the winds raged until the failing light of day turned to darkness.

The kind of darkness that cackles.

The kind of darkness that has claws.

At the centre of the storm sat a ring of ancient stones. Once upon a time, there had been many such circles but there were only a few left. For thousands of years the stones had slept: just a small collection of mossy rocks forgotten by everyone except the sort of people who think magic is all about wearing robes made out of old curtains and prancing about. Most of the stones had fallen and cracked, but their ancient magic still worked. And now the circle was awake. Strange shadows danced on the snow around them. Weird black and purple lights flickered.

Between two of the standing stones, red eyes opened. A hooded creature stepped out of darkness and into the world, its tattered cloak swirling in the gale.

Lifting a hand, it stared for a moment at its own skeleton fingers, then up at the boiling sky above. *"Yesssss,"* it said. "It issss time. Time for sssssuffering and pain."

A frying pan caught it full in the face with a *cloinnng* sound that echoed off the stones.

"You ain't wrong there Mister Ghoulie," screeched a voice.

"Ooooo *lovely,* Dot," shrieked another as the ghoul collapsed in a heap of rags.

Two elderly witches cackled as their brooms swooped to a halt. Boots crunched in the snow as they dismounted.

"You sure it's a ghoul. Looks like a wraith to me Dot," said Enid, a hunchbacked crone with a toothless face like a ball of dried chewing gum. "I never could tell the difference though."

"No, that's a ghoul, my dear. Wraiths are more wispy around the edges," said Dot, who was equally as old and bent and as disgusting to look at as an old man's underwear. "Let's make sure it's deaded, eh?"

"Shall we go through its pockets first?"

"Nah, they never has anything worth pinching Enid."

The ghoul stirred. *"Foolssss,"* it hissed, climbing to its

skeleton feet. "You cannot kill that which doesss not live."

The two witches glanced at each other. "It don't know us very well, does it Enid?" said Dot.

"No Dot," replied the second witch, cracking her knuckles. "I reckon we'm be pretty good at killing that what does not live."

"Only one way to find out Enid."

A few minutes later the two old witches were jumping up and down on a heap of definitely-very-dead rags.

"You know what Dot," said Enid as she gave the ghoul a just-to-make-sure kick.

"What's that then my old poppet?"

"I thinks I'm going to enjoy this war."

"Oh yes ducks," sniggered Dot. "I always did say that you can't beat giving the undead creatures of the nightmare pit a right good kicking. Or clowns. I does love punching a clown. Anyway, what do you say we puts the boot in one last time?"

"Heh, heh, heh," cackled Enid. "You knows me so well dearie," she said. "Alright then, there's a couple of bones which ain't completely pulverised yet."

Bing bong.

The noise came from deep inside Enid's dress.

"Yer mobile's ringing Enid," said Dot.

Reaching into a pocket, Enid pulled out a crystal ball the size of a tennis ball. Both witches leaned over and peered into it. Pressed up against the glass from the inside was a face that looked as though it had been reflected in the back of a spoon. The face of Blanche Nightly, ghost-hunter.

"This is Spectre to Hag Squadron Two," said Blanche's tiny voice. "Come in Hag Two."

"This is Hag Two," croaked Enid. "Go ahead Spectre."

"The spirits report werewolves breaking through at Stonehenge. Squadrons Three, Seventeen and Twenty are moving in. Looks like a big one."

"On our way," cackled Enid, slipping the crystal ball back into her pocket. "Werewolves Dot. They say you needs a silver bullet to kill a werewolf."

"They only says that because they ain't thought to try a frying pan, Enid my sweet."

The two crones mounted their broomsticks and flew back into the howling gale, black cloaks streaming in the wind and their cackles blowing across the frozen landscape. Behind them, the heap of rags was completely still. In the centre of the stone circle, however, a new pair of red eyes blinked open. Then another. And another.

1
The Prisoner in the Tower

Black magic curled like ink through water, poisoning everything it touched, freezing the world into a deathly mid-winter. At the heart of the darkness stood the Bleak Fortress – *exactly* the kind of half-ruined, turrety, dark, and brooding castle you would expect to find on a jagged mountain top in Transylvania. Wind moaned around crumbling battlements. Snow and ice battered stained grey walls. Bats burst from a broken tower, only to turn around and head back inside, where it was slightly less cold. Hanging upside down beneath the rafters, they wrapped themselves in leathery wings and went "brrrr," very quietly.

A light shone in an arched window high up in a tower that was only slightly crooked. The window looked in on a prison. It would be nice to say that it was a cold, dark dungeon with chains on the wall and rusty machines with nails in, but in fact it was a warm, comfortable room, with soft carpet, a crackling fire and flickering candles. Nevertheless, it was a prison.

Inside, a young girl paced up and down as well as she could while wearing an extremely tight dress of black velvet. This made her pacing up and down more like taking tiny mouse steps but it was helping her to think, and that was the important thing.

Wherever Sam stepped frogs hopped out of the way. With her foot, Sam gently nudged one under a huge wooden bed that had been carved with ghastly gibbering demons. She took a deep breath. "OK Ringo," she said to a beetle who was doing star jumps on an equally ghastly chest of drawers. "We're not doing so well with the whole witch-war, saving-the-world thing, so pay attention."

The beetle stopped exercising and looked up.

"These are our most urgent problems," she said, holding up a finger. "Number one. Evil, power-crazed sorceress Diabolica Nightshade is turning the world to darkness, making it winter forever and setting free all the dreaded creatures of the night. On the night of the Midwinter Moon she is going to crown herself Wicked but Lovely Witch Queen of All the World. All of this is very bad."

She paused in her pacing for a moment, glancing at her familiar to make sure he was paying attention.

3

"Two," she continued, "my best friend is in the dungeons and will be tortured if I disobey Diabolica or even *think* about doing any magic. Again, this is the opposite of good."

"Three. Our only friends are a bunch of very confused old women and Esmelia Sniff, who won't think twice about betraying us if it serves her own wicked plans, or if she just happens to feel like it. Once more, this is bad."

"Four," Sam grumped, throwing herself onto the ghastly, but surprisingly squashy, bed. "This is a really stupid dress for pacing up and down in. It must have been designed by Stupidity Stupid of the Stupid Dress Company. It's like being squeezed into a sausage skin."

Ringo gestured with his front legs.

"Good idea, thanks," panted Sam. Laying back, she wriggled until the dress was bunched up around the top of her thighs. She crossed her legs with a sigh of relief. One of the seams burst with a ripping sound and a couple of diamond buttons popped off. "I don't know why I can't just wear jeans," Sam moaned. "Even old trout-face Esmelia let me wear jeans."

With a clatter of beetle wings, Ringo flew onto her knee and looked up at her.

"Anyway, what was I saying… oh yes… We need a plan Ringo. Any ideas? I was thinking we should try and steal my wand back then, you know, undo all Diabolica's wickedness."

With the thought of The White Wand of… Oi You Could Have Someone's Eye Out With That, Sam scowled. She'd risked her life to make it, but Esmelia had stolen it from her a few moments later and then Diabolica had taken it. Now it had been hidden from her. Even so, Sam could feel the gentle fizz of its magic. The White Wand of… Oi You Could Have Someone's Eye Out With That was somewhere in the Bleak Fortress, and it was calling to her.

The beetle patted her knee gently.

Sam realised she'd been staring at the wall. "What?" she said, blinking and trying to push the faint magical buzzing of her wand to the back of her mind. "Have you thought of something?"

Ringo rose into the air and buzzed around the room. He came to a stop an inch from the end of Sam's nose and hovered there.

"Go and find help? In this weather? Are you mad? Absolutely not Ringo, you'd never make it through the storm."

Landing on the tip of a polished wooden demon's horn at the end of the bed, Ringo looked up at her and flexed his tiny muscles.

"Yes, I know you've been working out," Sam replied. "You're in great shape. If I had to pick any beetle to fly thousands of miles through a blizzard, it would definitely be you." She pointed at the wind-blasted snow out of the window. "But look at it out there. You'd freeze to death in seconds."

Ringo flicked a leg, waving away Sam's objections.

She peered at the beetle, her green eyes thoughtful in the dim firelight. "I know you're brave Ringo, but the answer's 'no'. We have to do *something* though. If I just had my wand…"

On the duvet, Ringo clicked his pincers sulkily.

Sam ignored him. Somewhere in the Bleak Fortress The White Wand of… Oi You Could Have Someone's Eye Out With That was calling to her again. A silly, dreamy look crossed her face. "If I just had my wand I could crush Diabolica like a bug," she muttered.

Ringo crossed his front legs and tapped his back foot.

The look left Sam's face abruptly. She blushed. "Sorry… I meant like a grape, or something else easily crushed. A cream bun maybe. Definitely not a bug."

After a moment of embarrassed silence, Sam gasped in excitement. "You're right though Ringo," she whispered. "Someone's got to get out of here, but it doesn't have to be *you*. We'll rescue Helza. Yes, that's it! I'll use magic. I can magic her anywhere in the world just like *that*." She snapped her fingers.

Ringo raised his wings unhappily.

"Yes, Diabolica will punish me," Sam breathed. "Of course she will. But what's the worst she can do? Keep me prisoner in the Bleak Fortress? Tell me to go to my room and think about what I've done?"

She paused for a moment, then said, "Not even Diabolica would hurt her own daughter, would she?"

Ringo looked uncertain.

"Well, she might, but it would be worth it." Having decided that she couldn't care less about what punishments might be in store, words tumbled out of Sam's mouth. "Helza will be safely away from the torture chamber," she babbled. "*And* she can take a message for us, to Esmelia and the crones… I know, I know, Esmelia can't be trusted but she really *hates* Diabolica. She won't be able to stop herself coming and trying to give her another black eye. And while Diabolica's got her hands full with Esmelia we can find The White Wand of…

Oi You Could Have Someone's Eye Out With That. Then we can cause Diabolica some *serious* trouble. It's brilliant Ringo. Brilliant. They'll probably write a book about how clever you are. Well done."

Ringo looked confused. This had not been his plan at all. His plan had involved being the brave and heroic beetle of the hour, flying through snow and ice to fetch help. Nevertheless, he rather liked the idea of someone writing a book about him, especially if it were called something like *Ringo: Beetle of Destiny.* Quickly, he decided that it would have a close-up of him on the cover, looking serious and clever. For a moment he wondered if he should wear glasses. Everyone looks clever in glasses. Possibly a hat too.

"Well, what are we waiting for? Let's go get Helza out," said Sam, interrupting Ringo's thoughts of bookish fame. Holding up her skirts, she ran for the door, stopped and ran back to the chest of drawers. Opening the bottom one she said, "On second thoughts, I'm not rescuing anyone dressed like this."

2

Misery Hates Company

The snowstorm raged on, like bad interference on a TV set. Miles from anywhere, hidden by leg-breakingly steep hills, specks of golden light glowed in the white wasteland. The Goblin's Elbow, the hotel for magical folk, was a tiny haven of warmth in a freezing world.

In hotel's cosy bar – all polished brass and dark wood and well-stuffed sofas – Esmelia Sniff, wicked witch, threw herself into a chair. Her cat, Tiddles, jumped onto her lap. Clutching the chair's arms with bent and stained old fingers, Esmelia rocked furiously. She'd spent long years rocking back and forth in the chair by the fire in her old cottage in Pigsnout Wood. Now, rocking was just something she did without even thinking about it, like picking her nose and scratching her armpits. Unfortunately, she wasn't in her old cottage and the chair she had sat in wasn't a rocking chair. This became clear when it failed to rock. Instead, it tipped forward, throwing Esmelia and Tiddles head-first into the fireplace.

"I done that on purpose," she screeched quickly, scrabbling about on the floor and thrashing at the hissing, spitting Tiddles with a flaming pointy hat.

No-one answered. At the bar, a group of spangly-hatted wizards and Lionel Ulcer, the landlord, clamped their lips together and held their breath. Suddenly, they all seemed very interested in a small crack in the ceiling.

A short, beardless, apprentice wizard called Wolfbang Pigsibling made an accidental noise with his mouth and was immediately nudged black and blue by the wizards around him.

Esmelia narrowed her eyes until they were just tiny slits in a maze of warty wrinkles and glared a glare that could have dropped a charging rhinoceros.

"Something *funny?*" she asked quietly.

On curly-toed slippers, the gaggle of wizards shuffled away from the purple-faced apprentice. Wolfbang stuffed a fist into his treacherous mouth. Eyes popping with fear, he was caught, alone, in the blast of Esmelia's glare. "Mmmf mmm mmmmff," the young wizard replied.

"You seems to have yer knuckles caught in yer teeth," said Esmelia with soft menace. "If I was you, I'd get lost before it's *my* knuckles."

Choking, the apprentice fled for the door.

Glaring at the remaining wizards one after another, Esmelia whispered, "Anyone else think me checking up the chimney was a teensy bit amusin'?"

The wizards shook their heads, dislodging morsels of breakfast from their beards.

Muttering under her breath, Esmelia sat in a different chair. She was not in a good mood. She hadn't, in fact, been in a good mood her entire life. Being born in a ditch had put her in a sulky frame of mind right from the start and she'd never really perked up since. As she peered around for a something to throw at the wall a large frog hopped onto a coffee table and gave her a damp stare. Esmelia's fingers twitched but, despite her dreadful mood, she decided that splatting Cakula von Drakula, the Most Superior High and Wicked Witch, on the wallpaper probably wasn't a good idea. For a start, Lionel Ulcer would try and make her pay for cleaning the stain. "You can stop lookin' at me like that you slimy little pest," she scowled instead. "It ain't my fault you're still all befrogginated."

Frogs don't have eyebrows, so the frog didn't raise one. It blinked slowly instead.

Esmelia remembered that if she hadn't swapped Cakula for an ordinary frog in order to trick her apprentice, Cakula would, by now, have been turned back into a vampire-witch. "Alright, it *is* my fault you're still befrogginated," she continued. "But there ain't much you can do about it, so hop it before I splashes you all over the wall."

The frog gave her a last stare. With a tiny shrug, it hopped over the side of the coffee table and disappeared under a sideboard. Harrumphing in an overly harrumphy way, Esmelia threw herself back in the chair and glared at nothing.

The old witch never really needed a reason to be in a foul mood, but today she had one.

There was a war among witches, and she was stuck.

As the acting Most Superior High and Wicked Witch she should be screaming through the skies on a broomstick, ordering everyone about and breaking a few legs.

Instead, she was stuck at the Goblin's Elbow. Trapped with a bunch of useless wizards. While power-crazed evil sorceress Diabolica Nightshade spread her evil and plunged the world into neverending winter all Esmelia could do was stamp about the hotel, cursing and generally making everyone's life a misery. Nothing could travel through the thick snow outside on foot. She'd tried to make herself a new broomstick, but it was a long and difficult spell and Esmelia was the type of witch who went in for meddling and being nasty and occasionally giving people a black eye, rather than actual magic. It hadn't been a success. Every broom at the Goblin's Elbow, as well as the vacuum cleaner, had exploded. Esmelia had even tried sitting on a toilet brush and shouting "giddy-up" but that had been a total disaster, too. The tiny plastic broomstick had spun round her bedroom three times before diving into the toilet with a screaming Esmelia still on board. And *then* it had exploded.

"I've got *meddling* to do," Esmelia shouted, pounding a fist on the arm of the chair. "And being

nasty. Black eyes also. Why can't none of you useless wizards magic me up a broom?"

"My dear Esmelia, wizards don't ride *brooms*," gasped Professor Sebastian Dentrifice, tugging on his beard nervously. *"Brooms* are strictly for the ladies. Wizards have more cunning means of getting about. We move through the world on mysterious pathways and shadowy tracks, disappearing from one place and appearing somewhere quite different."

"You mean you *walk,*" Esmelia replied.

"That's right, we walk. It gets you there eventually and it's jolly good for the figure too," said Dentrifice brightly, slapping his enormous stomach.

"Ain't no good when it's ten feet of snow out though, is it?"

"Snow is nature's way of telling you to stay indoors and get all comfy," replied Dentrifice with a wink. "And talking of getting comfy, how about dinner tonight? Maybe a little dancing. Who knows where it might end."

"I knows where it'd end," snapped Esmelia. "It'd end with blood pouring out your nose."

Professor Dentrifice appeared not to have heard. "Just you and I," he whispered, "candlelight and soft music..."

"Oh shut yer trap," interrupted Esmelia. "If you ain't noticed, that meddling Dimlybillica Nightspade's gone and plunged the world into neverending winter."

"Oh, never mind about *that,*" replied the Professor with a light wave. "They do that every now and again, those witches. In a hundred years or so some young hero will come along and vanquish her. In the meantime, we'll stay here, tucked up all cosy."

Esmelia scratched her armpit. She had to admit it wasn't the neverending winter and the world taking over that she minded. The wizard was right about that: it was perfectly acceptable behaviour for a witch. What really got up her hooked, bent and warty nose was that Diabolica had burned her cottage down, stolen her apprentice, and nearly turned her into an earwig. Plus, the evil sorceress had made her look like a complete fool by beating her in a magical duel while Esmelia had been wearing only her underwear.

Taking over the world and plunging it into neverending winter was perfectly understandable, but *nobody* made Esmelia Sniff look like a fool. She burned for revenge. "What kind of a witch would I be if I didn't beat her to a jelly with her own arms?" she muttered.

"A *happy* witch?" asked Dentrifice.

"Don't you dare use the 'h' word round me. Disgustin' language," Esmelia spat. "Flippin' wizards, what are you good for anyway? Eh?"

"Umm, we're quite good at fireballs actually."

"Bah, fireballs," sneered Esmelia. "What else?"

"Erm... great balls of fire," replied Dentrifice.

"Huuuge flaming globes," said Old Harry "Wooden" Legg.

Silence fell. "Fireballs good," mumbled Old Harry eventually. "Fireballs go ka-*boom.*"

Esmelia glared at him. Old Harry wisely stopped talking and stared down at his fingernails. "Oh, just get lost, the lot of you," she screeched. "I can't think with you lot bein' all useless at me. And I needs to think. I needs a *plot.*"

"I think that was definitely a 'yes' for dinner, don't you Harry?" Professor Dentrifice muttered as the wizards shuffled towards the door.

Sitting stiffly, Esmelia scowled even more deeply. She missed her rocking chair. She missed her cottage with its lumpy walls and sagging straw roof, the smell of mouse poo and the rusty cauldron bubbling away in the corner. And she missed her apprentice…

"No, I doesn't miss *her,*" Esmelia whispered. "I just misses bein' *nasty* to her. I misses the look on her little face when I tells her to clean out the cat's litter tray. Besides, she's *my* apprentice. An apprentice is an apprentice and that's the law."

Esmelia glared angrily out of the window, across a white landscape where snow piled higher and higher.

"I think," she said eventually. "I needs a cauldron."

3

The Witches are Watching

Sam had never been the type of girl to sit in front of a mirror with a pair of curling tongs, and, at Esmelia's cottage she had happily worn stains and patches on her clothes and several layers of dirt. Occasionally, she would rinse her hair in a bucket of rainwater or, on a nice day, take a dip in a woodland pool, but since the bucket was usually full of newts and woodland pools are more mud than water she hadn't been what you might call "clean" for some time. When Diabolica had brought her to the Bleak Fortress, however, she'd been hosed down, scraped, scoured, scrubbed, sandpapered, and scented. Her hair had been trimmed and washed, conditioned and styled. She'd been pushed and bullied into dresses. And she definitely hadn't been allowed to wear the pointy hat Esmelia had given her. Diabolica had been very clear on the subject. Pointy hats, she had said, were strictly for the type of crone who hadn't read a fashion magazine since bandy legs and oozing facial pustules were all the rage.

Sam had hated every moment, but with Helza in the dungeons she'd had to do as she was told.

Now, she burrowed through drawers frantically, throwing brand new, hideously expensive, dresses over her shoulder without a thought. Her eyes gleamed with excitement.

After a few moments, she stopped rummaging. Screwed up at the back of the drawer were her own clothes: warm vest, black jumper, black jeans, scuffed sneakers, and a black pointed hat, squashed flat.

"Much better," she whispered to herself. "Comfy."

Ringo politely turned his back as Sam pulled the sausage skin dress over her head with more ripping noises and grabbed the vest. As she did so, a small roll of ancient Egyptian papyrus dropped onto the carpet. Watched only by Ringo's sharp beetle eyes, it rolled under the chest of drawers.

After pulling on jeans and a jumper, Sam gently lifted Esmelia's second best hat. Being crushed up inside a drawer hadn't done it any favours. As well as being patched and battered and held together with Sam's not-particularly-brilliant sewing it now flopped over to one side. With a smile she settled it on her head.

Turning to Ringo, she whispered, "Let's go."

Sam's door creaked open a crack. The passageway outside was much less warm and inviting than her room. Torches hung from the walls, spluttering in the drafts and lighting bare stone hung with cobwebs. Opposite her door, a dusty portrait of Murderina Moldblatter (Most High and Superior Wicked Witch 1642–1699) sneered down at her over a nose that could have been used as a pickaxe.

Pausing for a moment, Sam listened carefully. The only sounds were the wind whistling through cracks in the wall and faint sound of shivering bats. "Which way Ringo?" she whispered. Helza would be in a dungeon somewhere, but the Bleak Fortress was famous for having more dungeons than toilets. Most of the guest rooms even had their own small, *en suite* jail cells.

There was only one place where Diabolica would put a prisoner though, and Sam had started to understand how her mother's mind worked. "What do you think? Deepest, darkest, dreariest dungeon?" she said softly.

Ringo clicked in reply.

A grin appeared on Sam's face. Dressed in her own clothes and on a mission to rescue her friend, she felt like herself again. In fact, she felt even better than usual. For once she was doing something without Esmelia Sniff glaring over her shoulder, chewing her own gums and telling her she was a "peskilential little maggot" in an annoyingly screechy voice.

Keeping to the shadows, Sam slipped away.

At the end of the corridor a spiral staircase wound down into the darkness. Keeping guard at the top was a life-size painting of Lady Cursula McStabbish (Most High and Superior Wicked Witch 1798–1823), her hand raising a triumphant pickled onion to the heavens. Touching the cold stones of the wall to guide herself, Sam stepped down carefully, her boots making no sound.

The staircase led to another corridor. Torches burned brightly here, enormous drippy candles adding their own light. Sam was close to the Great Throne Room. Holding her breath, she ran. After a few yards later, her shoes squeaked to a halt on polished stone. In the distance, she heard the unmistakable sound of dragging footsteps.

Hardly daring to breathe, she slipped behind a statue of Pandora Box (Most High and Superior Wicked Witch 1905–1952), and waited. Seconds later, two of Diabolica's zombie-witches appeared at the end of the

corridor, faces slack and bloodshot, blank eyes bulging. As they came closer, one turned to the other and groaned, "Di-a-bol-i-caaaa."

"Di-a-bol-i-ca," the other agreed.

Hunched behind Pandora's back (which, by chance, was also hunched), Sam waited until they had disappeared round the corner before sprinting away towards another staircase.

As she ran, the eyes in a portrait of Petunia "Potty" Mouth (Most High and Superior Wicked Witch 1868–1871) swivelled to follow. Behind the painting, another voice droned "Di-a-bol-i-ca."

Into crooked passages Sam and Ringo crept, always heading downwards and slowly making their way to the lowest parts of the fortress. With every new passage the portraits and statues became older, each witch more repulsive and warty than the last. Eventually, massive stone walls gave way to roughly carved rock. The last statue was so old that the witch's face had crumbled away. The worn carving said that the hooded crone holding a basket of plump apples was Gruselda the Skanky (Most Superior High and Wicked Witch 934–997). One last torch burned by the statue. Ahead was only darkness. With a shiver, Sam lifted the bundle of burning sticks and continued into the gloom.

The flame was burning low by the time she found the deepest, darkest, dreariest dungeon. Lifting the torch she looked around in its weak light. Ahead, an arch led into a circular chamber with chains on the wall. It was absolutely stuffed with rusty machines with nails in. Around the walls were a row of doors heavy wooden doors, each studded with metal. All had a small barred window, because every jailer loves peering in at his prisoners.

Stepping into the middle of the chamber, she called gently, "Helza? Are you here?"

There was rustling noise. A face appeared at the bars of the furthest door. A face that was as dirty and streaked with tears as Sam's was clean. "Hey bud," she croaked. "Hair's looking good. No twigs and, hey, you've had a trim."

"Helza!" Sam shrieked, tears of joy pricking her eyes. Dodging past the torture machines, she lifted the torch, stood on her tip-toes and peered through the bars. Behind Helza, a chained skeleton grinned at her. The cell was small and damp with just a thin heap of straw for a bed. An untouched bowl contained something that looked as though it had come straight from Esmelia's kitchen, possibly by way of the cat's bottom. "I'm sorry," Sam said quietly, reaching through the bars to touch the tear-stained face that peered out. "So sorry I took so long."

"Not your fault," replied Helza, shrugging and attempting a smile. "Anyway, it's a hell hole but the rats have been keeping me company."

A fresh tear trickled down Helza's cheek.

"It's over now," Sam whispered firmly. "I'm going to magic you out of here. Can you take a message to Esmelia? To the other witches?"

"No way amigo," Helza shot back. "If you magic me away, Diabolica will kill you. No way."

"No she won't, I'm her daughter. She'll find a way to punish me but she won't *hurt* me. And whatever she does, it'll be worth it if you're safe. Besides, we're at *war*. We have to take the risk."

"Can't you magic both of us out of here?"

"It doesn't work like that."

Helza thought about it. "Well OK," she said eventually. "What's the message?"

"Tell her that all she has to do is get here and keep Diabolica busy while I find The White Wand of... Oi You Could Have Someone's Eye Out With That. I'll do the rest."

"But you know what Esmelia's like: moody and that. What if she tells me to get lost?"

"If she gets to poke Diabolica in the eye, she'll do it."

Helza thought about it. Eventually, she said, "OK then. I'll be back as soon as I can but keep yourself safe while I'm gone."

"You take care too. Ready? Here we go."

Taking a deep breath, Sam reached out for the magic she would need to send Helza across more than a thousand miles to the Goblin's Elbow. She didn't have to look very far. There was magic all around her, flooding out of the Bleak Fortress and into the world.

Bad magic.

Choking, Sam stumbled backwards, goosebumps breaking out along her arms. This wasn't like any magic she'd used before. It was dark as a Science teacher's heart. It tasted like acid.

But she had no choice. With a creeping chill of terror, Sam pulled the magic to her again. This time, she nearly threw up. Normally, magic made her blood fizz pleasantly. Now she felt as if her body had been filled with angry wasps.

Stop being so feeble! she scolded herself, steadying her feet and trying again.

There was power in the darkness. Sam could feel its icy glamour. She tried to think only of the spell, but the magic whispered to her. Whispered about secrets and strength and knowledge. She felt the tug of wickedness; the limitless possibilities of the night; the delights of evil.

Her eyes closed. A chilly smile flickered on her lips.

The wasps stopped.

"Are you alright bud, you don't look so good." To Sam, Helza's voice was muffled, a million miles away.

The darkness chuckled.

Helza's voice again: "Ringo, it's gone wrong. Do something."

Sharp beetle pincers dug into the skin of Sam's neck, causing a sharp jab of pain. Sam's eyes fluttered open. "No… no. I *can't!*" she yelled, dropping to her knees and gasping for air. Her stomach heaved.

"Sam… Sam! What's the matter? What's going… oooooh *NO!*"

There was a shuffling sound behind her. Sam felt herself being lifted by the armpits.

"Di-a-bol-i-caaaa," a voice moaned by her ear.

"Di-a-bol-i-ca," agreed another.

4
Book Burning

Diabolica, also known as "Deadly", Nightshade looked up from the book in her lap as the massive doors of the Bleak Fortress's Great Throne Room flew open. "Oh *there* you are dear," she said in a voice like melting chocolate as Sam was dragged before her by the two shuffling zombie-witches.

"Di-a-bol-i-caa," groaned one, letting go of Sam's arm. False teeth slipped out of its mouth and clattered to the floor.

Relaxing in the carved throne of The Most Superior High and Wicked Witch as if it was a sun-lounger, Diabolica tapped The Black Wand of Ohh Please Don't Turn Me Into Aaaarghh... Ribbett against her cheek. "And you've come dressed as a tramp," she continued. "Really, Samantha, you're turning out to be a terrible disappointment."

Sam clenched her teeth, hating Diabolica at the same time as a small part of her squirmed with shame. A part that wanted to beg forgiveness and be wrapped up

29

in her mother's arms. A part that couldn't bear being a disappointment to such a beautiful, powerful mother. Not trusting herself to speak, Sam gave Diabolica a glare that would have made Esmelia proud.

"Tsk, if I had a penny for every person who's ever glared at me like that… well, I'd have eight pounds and ninety-four pence by now darling. It *really* doesn't work you know. See how not scared I am. Marvel as I fail to shake with fear."

The glare turned into a scowl. Like many young girls before her Sam found that it was easier to be angry than try and make sense of her feelings.

"So, what am I going to do with you, young lady?" Diabolica sighed. She glanced down at the book. Sam recognised it as *Think Yourself Witch: 101 Steps Towards Becoming a Crone,* a book that was haunted by the ghost of Lilith Dwale, her grandmother and Diabolica's mother. "Any ideas Lilith?" Diabolica asked the pages.

As Diabolica stared at the book, blood rushed to her cheeks. A sudden flash of fury crossed her brow as Lilith's words crawled across the page. In less than a second it was gone, replaced by a sneering smile. "Oh, I don't think I'd want to do *that* Lilith," Diabolica said. "I like my bottom just the way it is thank you."

Closing the book with a thump, Diabolica looked up at Sam again.

"I told you what would happen if I caught you doing magic, didn't I?" she said firmly. "Your friend in the dungeon is going to suffer for this. Rules are rules."

"No," Sam gasped. "Please don't hurt Helza. I wasn't... That is, I was just... I... I'm s-sorry mother. I didn't mean to."

"Oh *please,*" interrupted Diabolica, rising from the throne and stepping towards her daughter. "Do you think I can't recognise a pesky plot-foiler when I see one?"

"It wasn't like that. I was just..."

Diabolica raised a hand to silence her. "So you *weren't* attempting to rescue your friend? And you *definitely* weren't trying to stop me becoming Wicked but Lovely Witch Queen of All the World?" Diabolica's green eyes burned into Sam's.

"No, I..." Sam began, and then stopped. She pressed her lips together.

After a moment, Diabolica said, "That's what I thought. The trouble with you saving-the-world types is you're no good at lying. No good at all."

Sam gazed up at her mother with hatred in her eyes.

"I just want to go home," she whispered.

Diabolica laughed. "What, back to picking woodlice out of your hair in that rat-infested dump in the forest? And that *repulsive* Sniff baggage?"

"Yes. I was happy there."

Diabolica's eyebrow twitched.

"Alright, not happy as such. Happy*ish*. When Esmelia wasn't around. But it was home. Everything was simple when all I had to do was clean out the cat's litter tray. It was where I belonged."

"Wrong, wrong, wrong," said Diabolica. "You belong here. With me. Your mother." She paused for a moment, then said, "Besides, I seem to remember burning Esmelia's cottage to the ground."

Sam's shoulders sagged. She had to admit that Diabolica had a point. She could never go back to her comfortable attic room in Esmelia's creaking old cottage. Those days were gone. Even the power of the two wands couldn't turn back time and bring the lumpy old cottage back. "That doesn't mean I have to stay here with you," she muttered sulkily.

"Wrong again," snapped Diabolica. "Believe me, I'm not terribly happy about it either but, like it or not, you *are* my daughter. More importantly, you're quite powerful and have an annoying habit of trying to foil my plans. Do you really think I'm stupid enough to let you out of my sight?"

"What harm can I do you when you have both wands?"

"Pah. You do-gooders always come up with something if you get half a chance. No, you'll stay right here and, one way or another, you'll join me."

"What do you mean?" asked Sam.

"In one week from now the moon will be full," answered Diabolica, shaking her mane of dark hair. "All the dreaded creatures of the night will kneel before me. At midnight I will crown myself Wicked but Lovely Witch Queen of All the World. And then I will turn my beasts and my monsters and my zombie army loose. Across the world, people will learn the meaning of *fear.*"

"Yes, I *know,*" scowled Sam. "You've been telling me this fifty times a day."

"Well, what I haven't told you is that if you don't join me by then, I'll *make* you join me."

Sam's head snapped up, her face pale. "You don't mean…?" she said, glancing over her shoulder at the zombie witches. One of them was now trying to squeeze a set of false teeth up its nose. Feeling eyes upon it, the zombie stopped for a moment and droned *"teeef."*

"Mmm hmm," murmured her mother, nodding gently. "One way or another you'll learn to love your mummy. Even if I have to turn you into a shuffling, drooly thing." She smiled brightly. "To be honest, I don't think I'll notice the difference. All you do is mope about the place looking like death warmed up anyway."

"You can't do that to me, I'm *family.*"

Diabolica leaned over Sam until their noses were almost touching. "Well start acting like it then," she hissed sharply. "I'm fed up to the back teeth with all this namby-pamby, do-goodery rubbish." Diabolica started squeaking in a high-pitched voice. "Oooo don't hurt Helza mummy. Don't take over the world. It's *eeeevil.* Let's be nice to everyone and dance about singing fa-la-la-la-la." Diabolica paused for a moment, and then finished, "Pa-the-tic."

Colour returned to Sam's face in a rush as anger returned. "You *are* evil," she snapped.

"Everyone needs a hobby dear," Diabolica shrugged. Standing straight again, she sneered. "And, by the way, this is what I think of *family.*"

In one movement, Diabolica heaved *Think Yourself Witch* into the Great Throne Room's enormous fireplace.

"And *your* bottom too, Lilith Dwale," she shouted as flames instantly caught at the old paper.

"Grandmother!" With a scream, Sam lunged towards the fireplace, hands stretched out to save the book.

Diabolica's elegant fingers caught her by the back of her jumper, pulling her back. Sam thrashed and struggled as her grandmother's book blazed, spouting ashes towards the ceiling. But Diabolica was surprisingly strong; she could only watch, sobbing as her precious book burned.

"I *hate* you," Sam shrieked.

Diabolica stared at the fire, a satisfied smile on her face. "Really dear?" she said. "Excuse me while I quiver with terror."

When *Think Yourself Witch* had been reduced to a black heap of wafer-thin cinders Sam stopped struggling. A few flakes of ash fell around her. She caught one and peered down at it through her tears.

Faintly, tiny words appeared: *Be nasty.*

The ash crumbled to dust in her hand. Sam closed her fingers around it.

Diabolica was still gazing at the flames and hadn't noticed. "Really, I don't know why Esmelia put up with you," she said. "She may be a ridiculous, wart-faced old newt-botherer but at least she think she doesn't go around being *nice*. If you were a proper witch and not a rather boring little girl who just happens to be quite good with magic, you'd know it's all about being *nasty*."

Ice clutched Sam's soul. "I am *not* boring," she said softly.

Diabolica snorted.

"And if you want to see nasty, I'll show you nasty."

"Huh, you couldn't if you tried," Diabolica purred.

This time, Sam didn't have to look for the dark magic. This time it was waiting for her.

Blackness rushed through her blood. Her heartbeat thumped. Sam stepped back and let her eyes roll back in her head. Veins on her forehead throbbed purple as she raised her arms and gathered as much of the power as she could hold.

This time, she didn't feel sick. This time she felt *joyous*.

Holding her hands out towards Diabolica, she felt the blackness rise. With a snarl, she shrieked "Be *Gone,*" and cackled wildly as magic flooded from her fingertips towards her mother.

Covering a small yawn politely, Diabolica raised the The Black Wand of Ohh Please Don't Turn Me Into Aaaarghh… Ribbett with her spare hand and flicked

Sam's spell to one side. The blazing stream of purple and black magic smashed through the window and disappeared into the blizzard outside.

The gale whipped into the room in a blast of snow. Diabolica pushed blowing hair away from her face and looked at her daughter with a smile. "Not bad," she said after a moment. "Do try not to cackle though. It makes you sound ever-so-slightly like a lunatic. A simple 'mwah ha ha HA!' will do if you really have to."

"You… you tricked me," Sam gasped, as hair lashed at her face. "You made me angry on purpose. You wanted me to do that."

Diabolica smiled, her eyes shining with glee. "It's all about being *nasty* darling," she shouted above the storm. "Do try and keep up."

"I would never… never."

"Every time you use the dark magic it makes you just a little bit more wicked. Didn't it feel *good?*"

Anger was replaced by the sudden chill of shame. The dark magic *had* felt good. Better than good. And it had left her wanting more.

"Yes… no… I–I'm not like you. I'm not. I won't be evil. I just *can't.*"

"Ha, Esmelia taught you nothing," said Diabolica

softly. "But don't worry dear, it's never too late to learn. Now, why don't you go to your room and think about what you've done."

"Wait," Sam said urgently. "What about Helza?" You won't torture her will you?"

Diabolica's smile returned. She winked at Sam. "Rules are rules, dear," she said.

5
A Change of Heart

Tears ran down Sam's cheeks like wax dripping down a candle. Sitting on her demonic bed, she looked down through red eyes at her familiar and whispered hoarsely, "She's won, hasn't she Ringo? Diabolica's won. Helza will be tortured and unless I join my mother by the full moon I'll be a shuffling zombie with my knuckles dragging along the floor and dribble running down my chin."

Her beetle patted her knee and stroked his chin thoughtfully.

"What's worse is that a little bit of me *wants* to join her," Sam told him in a horrified whisper. "She's… well… she's my mother."

Ringo waved a leg in her face.

"No, you're right. I could never be like her. But I've got all this magical talent Ringo, and it's still not enough. I need my wand and Diabolica will never let me have it back."

Ringo crossed his front legs, making it plain that if

he could have tutted he would be tutting at this very moment. As beetles are not very good tutters, however, he had to make do with tapping one of his back legs impatiently.

Fresh tears began their journey down Sam's face. "What can I do without The White Wand of... Oi You Could Have Someone's Eye Out With That?" she sobbed.

For a moment, Ringo looked thoughtful, then he raised his leg again and made a complicated gesture.

"What? What are you talking about Ringo? How could I hope to beat Diabolica?"

Slowly, Ringo shook his tiny head.

"Well, yes I can do magic better than most but I'm nowhere near powerful enough to fight Diabolica and both wands." Her voice drifted off as she remembered the spell she had cast to make The White Wand of... Oi You Could Have Someone's Eye Out With That. *That* had been magic that no ordinary witch could have done. For a few seconds she had touched the magic that held the whole universe together. For a moment the whole of space and time had been hers and hers alone. The universe had spun around her in all its glory.

It had been pretty cool.

Her thoughts were interrupted by the beating of beetle wings. Ringo landed on her knee, a small scroll of ancient papyrus held between his pincers. With a bow, he dropped it.

The scroll rolled into Sam's lap.

She blinked in confusion. The little roll of old paper looked familiar, exactly like the spell for making a new wand that she had found in the tomb of the first witch. But that scroll was back in Blanche Nightly's cottage in Sawyer Bottom, thousands of miles away. Then she remembered. When she'd found it there had been another. She'd taken both, and then forgotten all about the second scroll in the excitement of making a new wand. It had been stuck in her vest ever since.

Frowning, Sam picked it up and carefully unrolled the ancient paper. Peering at it in the dim firelight, she recognised the words for

"wand", "destroy" and "warning: this spell may blow your brain out through your ears" in the Egyptian hieroglyphic writing. But she didn't need to read it: the picture in the middle of the papyrus spoke for itself. Like the spell that had made The Black Wand of Ohh Please Don't Turn Me Into Aaaarghh… Ribbett it showed a picture of a black wand. This time, however, it was broken, its magic dead.

Sam blinked again. In her hand was a spell that could destroy The Black Wand of Ohh Please Don't Turn Me Into Aaaarghh… Ribbett. Her thoughts whizzed about like morning bees.

Without the wand, Diabolica would be just a normal, everyday, power-crazed evil sorceress out to take over the world. Incredibly powerful, but not unbeatable.

If The Black Wand of Ohh Please Don't Turn Me Into Aaaarghh… Ribbett was destroyed, all Diabolica's spells would be broken. Cakula von Drakula would be debefrogginated.

Together, she and Cakula could easily beat Diabolica.

The surge of hope lasted two and a half seconds. "I-I can't do this spell Ringo," Sam stuttered. "What about The White Wand of… Oi You Could Have Someone's Eye Out With That? I'd destroy that too.

44

I could *never* do that. It's *my* wand."

Beetles may not be very good at tutting but they are surprisingly good at shrugging. They can do it with all six legs at once, which makes for a pretty amazing shrug. This shrug seemed to say, "What's the big deal? It's *only* a wand."

Sam took no notice. With a quick movement, she scrunched the scroll into a ball and tossed it across the room.

"No," she said flatly, crossing her arms. "I won't do it."

Ringo stared at her and then, looking weary, he waved a leg again.

"Hah," choked Sam, bitterly. "You might be right. At this stage anything *is* worth a try. And ever since I became a witch everyone's been telling me I should be nasty – Esmelia, Lilith, Diabolica… Maybe I should give *that* a try?"

Ringo fluttered his wings nervously. Suddenly, he didn't like the way this conversation was going.

"Maybe I should try being more like Esmelia, eh?" Sam continued. "Oh, I know she's a foul-tempered old hag with the brain of an ingrowing toenail. Yes, she's as mad as a hatter and she smells like a sick bag, but… but at least she's *not* boring." Pulling her knees up so that she could stare into Ringo's eyes, she hissed, "So maybe we should be asking ourselves: *what would Esmelia do?*"

Ringo knew what Esmelia would do. With one of his front legs, he scratched his armpit and picked his nose.

"Yes, but what *else?* She wouldn't muck about trying to rescue people – not Esmelia – she'd just be *nasty,* wouldn't she?"

Sam stared at the wall, tears drying on her cheeks, thoughts clicking like the locks on a dungeon door.

Ringo didn't like it at all.

For a long time, she sat silently. Then, in the gloom, Sam's green eyes flashed. She giggled.

Ringo took a step back. The giggle sounded suspiciously like a cackle.

"You know what," she said eventually. "I do believe that all this time I've been an utter and complete idiot."

Ringo took another step backwards. In the candlelight Sam looked exactly like Diabolica.

"I should have listened. Should have learned what every witch I know has been trying to teach me. I've been getting it all *wrong,*" Sam continued. "Being a witch isn't about being *good*. Being good is for people who look after broken down donkeys and help the old folks with their shopping. It's not for *witches.*"

Ringo waved four legs at her, trying to get her attention. Sam paid him no attention.

"I think, for once, I should try being a *proper* witch," she whispered.

She swept hair out of her face. Now her eyes were glinting with a look Ringo had never seen there before: a look of pure wickedness.

"I think I *should* try being nasty."

With a sudden movement Sam shuffled to the edge of the bed. Ringo was forced to jump off her knee. He buzzed his way up to his usual place on her shoulder.

Sam's fingers reached out and pulled on the window latch. Immediately, a bellow of wind roared into the room, knocking portraits of Diabolica off the wall and blowing out the candles. Snow began forming small drifts against the furniture. The gale snatched Esmelia's second-best hat from Sam's head. Her hair streamed back in the wind. "Winter's such a wonderful time of year," she murmured. "So refreshing."

Closing her eyes, Sam felt the dark magic swirling around the Bleak Fortress once more. It sang through her veins, telling her what it was to be evil. "I really am a very powerful witch, you know Ringo," she said dreamily. "Perhaps it's time that I showed everyone just how powerful. That wouldn't be boring, would it? Ringo…? *Ringo?*"

Sam craned her head around to look at her own shoulder where Ringo had been perched a few seconds before.

"Ringo!"

Sam felt no answering patter of tiny feet against her skin. The beetle was gone.

6

Pea and Ham Soup and Other Important Events

The ancient circle of Stonehenge. Witches hurtled out of the night, boots outstretched for balance, swinging frying pans like tennis champions. Here and there spells sizzled in the darkness. A werewolf raced across the landscape, its massive claws churning the snow, hungry fire in its eyes and its tongue lolling over deadly teeth. It was headed south, towards the Bleak Fortress and the heart of darkness. Diabolica was calling, and it obeyed. Soon it would be time to get into old ladies' beds with a frilly cap on its head, but first it had to go to its mistress.

A witch whistled.

The wolf looked up in surprise.

Cloooing-oing-oing.

With a whimper, the beast collapsed in the snow.

"Good boy. *Stay.*"

Bing bong. Bing bong.

Cursing under her breath, Enid pulled the mobile crystal ball from her pocket and peered down into

Blanche Nightly's fish face. "We're busy," she yelled over the driving wind. "Can't you text me?"

"The spirits say that something is coming," Blanche said calmly. "Tell the other squadrons and bring them back here."

"What? What's coming?"

For a moment, Blanche looked confused. "A hero," she said. "The spirits say that a hero is coming to lead us into the Bleak Fortress. We have to take the war to Diabolica."

"But what about these wolves? We're winning. We're actually winning."

"You're *not* winning. The monsters are coming through everywhere, you can slow a few of them down but you'll never stop them all. Let them go. Just come as quickly as you can."

"Can't I just get one more?"

Blanche Nightly sighed. "Alright, one more."

In the kitchen of the Goblin's Elbow, Esmelia Sniff bent over a bubbling cauldron and gave it an experimental stir. Squinting up at a huddle of wizards and Lionel Ulcer, she crowed, "Right wizard twonks, watch and learn. This is how a witch hatches a plot."

Lionel Ulcer's bald head with its wings of ginger hair bobbed. Playing nervously with his tie, he stuttered, "Y-You will be careful, won't you? That's a fresh batch of our famously thick pea and ham soup."

"Oooo my favourite," Esmelia said, dipping a ladle into the cauldron before the landlord could protest. She slurped a green mouthful, then spat it back in, with a "Bllleeeuuuuurgh." Wiping her mouth she said, "Disgustin'. What type of pee are you using? You wants some newt piddle in that. Adds a lovely tang does your newt piddle."

Lionel Ulcer squeezed his eyes closed so that he didn't have to look at the bubbles of Esmelia spit. In his head, he added the cost of a full cauldron of famously thick pea and ham soup to Esmelia's bill. After a second, he corrected himself and added it to Professor Dentrifice's bill instead. Esmelia, he had found, had a firm belief that all money belonged to her and no-one else should have any of it. Asking Esmelia to pay for anything was like asking his hair to grow back.

"What's she doing with a load of old soup?" asked apprentice wizard Wolfbang Pigsibling under his breath. "Doesn't seem very magic to me. Is she going to summon the demon War-Ming Broth, lord of Crouton?"

"Shush," shushed Professor Dentrifice, clipping his apprentice round the ear. "This is *educational.* Witches may *look* like brainless bundles of sweet, fluffy loveliness, but you watch: give a witch a cauldron and sooner or later she'll come up with a plot so dastardly it'll make your ears curl. Making spinning wheels fall asleep for a hundred years, getting handsome princes to marry seven dwarfs, and so on and so forth. Hatching plots over a bubbling cauldron is witchcrafting in action."

"Looks like a looney in action to me," muttered the apprentice staring at Esmelia.

Esmelia scowled across the room. "Seems to me some people are still flapping their lips when they should be watching and learning," she said.

"I was just telling young Pigsibling here about the wonder and magic of witchcraft my dear Esmelia," smiled the professor with a huge wink.

"Something wrong with your eye?" Esmelia snapped.

"No, I…"

"Well, there soon will be if you don't keep your gob shut," she interrupted, waving the ladle at him threateningly.

As the wizards muttered into silence, Esmelia gave

a low cackle, no more than a soft "meh heh heh heh herghh," and hunched so far over the cauldron that the hairs on her long and twisty warts almost touched the soup. The lights in the kitchen of the Goblin's Elbow dimmed. As the cackle faded out, the only sound was the *blop, blop, blopping* of boiling, famously thick, pea and ham soup.

Esmelia stirred it slowly.

"I've studied this. She'll start on the cackling and next is the mumbling," Professor Dentrifice whispered into Wolfbang's ear. "Then comes the plot."

Esmelia squinted across the rim of the cauldron, eyes glinting like angry currants. "Sorry," the professor said. "Don't mind me. Carry on, carry on."

The old witch returned to her work. The professor was right. With the cackling out of the way, she began mumbling about signs of upcoming doom and disaster. These included hedgehogs being tetchy and the brindled cat falling down the back of the sofa. Next, as was also traditional, she made up a rhyme about the ingredients of her vile brew. This would have been more goosebumpy and skin crawly if the soup's ingredients had included poisoned snake guts, owl's wing, and frogs' toes instead of peas and ham. Nevertheless, Esmelia did her best, putting real effort into making, *"Simmer the bubbling brew of dread, and serve with a slice of crusty bread"* sound sinister.

The effort wasn't wasted. As he listened to the crone mumbling over the steaming green soup, a tingle of fear crept up Wolfbang Pigsibling's back like the fingers of a skeleton's hand. She might not be very good at magic, but the sight of Esmelia hunched, squinting and mumbling over a steaming green cauldron was enough to make anyone start thinking "Oh please, please, please don't let her be mumbling about *me."*

"Now the plot," whispered Professor Dentrifice tugging at his beard in excitement. "Look at her go, I'll bet it's a doozy."

The wizards held their breath as they waited.

And waited.

Esmelia squinted into the soup. At the best of times her face looked like the last balloon three days after a birthday party, but now new lines appeared among her wrinkles. To the untrained eye it looked as though her head was collapsing, but actually Esmelia was frowning.

Something was wrong.

A plot should have formed in her twisted, maggoty

brain. She should, at this very moment, have been rubbing her hands together and mumbling "Yes, yes, oooo that's a good plot that is. And that hat full of scorpions is a lovely touch. I'm a flippin' genius, that's what I am." Not once had she hatched plots over a bubbling cauldron and failed to come up with a scheme so devious and wicked that you could have dressed it in shorts and called it a gym teacher.

This time, there was nothing. Not even a hint of a plot. Esmelia stirred the cauldron again, faster this time, and squinted so hard it looked as though she was trying to squeeze her eyeballs out through her eyelids.

It didn't work. All she could see was a lonely chunk of ham going round and round on the surface.

Gritting both her teeth, she decided that desperate times called for desperate measures. More cackling was what was needed. Opening her mouth she began again, this time with a noise like a tractor starting: "Urrghh, uh uh uh, urgh-huuuuuurggh."

"Well this is a stroke of luck," hissed Professor Dentrifice, nudging the apprentice. "I do believe we're about to hear a real witch's cackle Pigsibling. Don't start biting your fingernails; by the time she's finished you'll have chewed 'em up to the elbow."

"Neeeeeeearghhehahaheugh," cackled Esmelia, stirring the cauldron so hard that famously thick pea and ham soup slopped over the rim. As she cackled the kitchen grew darker, and darker again. Crockery trembled on the shelves. Wolfbang Pigsibling found that his knees were knocking, as if trying to attract his attention. "Hello? Hello?" he could almost hear them shouting, "Anyone in? Can we get out of here please? Right now."

And still the cackle went on. When the terrified apprentice was certain that it couldn't get any worse, Esmelia managed to reach new depths of evil-soaked screech. "MEHEARRUURRRRCHEUUUGH," she cackled, sounding like a donkey in a food blender, and "EHHEHGUURUGGGH".

The cackle shook plates from the shelves and a flock of bats from the chimney until, abruptly, Esmelia stopped.

All was quiet apart from the knocking of Wolfbang Pigsibling's knees. Gradually the lights became brighter. The gaggle of wizards was pressed with their backs against the wall. A grey-faced Lionel Ulcer had picked up a wooden spoon and was trying to swat at bats swooping around his head. In his mind, he added some more, quite large, numbers to the professor's bill.

Unaware that the cost of his stay at the Goblin's Elbow had just gone up by several hundred pounds, Professor Dentrifice blinked once or twice and began clapping. "Bravo," he cried. *"Bravo* madam. What a cackle! You must have hatched a plot the likes of which has never been seen. Is it mind-bendingly cruel? Is it as wicked as a chainsaw in a bowl of porridge? Tell us. Tell us your black-hearted, spiteful plan."

Esmelia unhunched from over the cauldron. Her black dress was dripping with famously thick pea and ham soup. Her hat was floating in a puddle at the bottom of the cauldron. On her face was a look of pure fury.

Pausing only to dig a pea out of her ear with a faint popping noise, Esmelia gripped the rim of the cauldron and flung it out of the fireplace. Famously thick pea and ham soup spread in a slick among the broken plates.

"Don't just stand there you great scabby puddings," she croaked. "This cauldron isn't working. Bring me another."

Far above the earth, a tiny black shape was tossed around in the blizzard like a speck of fly poo in a washing machine. Tiny wings beat against the ice storm. Ringo was headed north, towards Britain and the distant Goblin's Elbow. That is, Ringo was *trying* to head north. Despite years of press-ups and star jumps and jogging, the beetle was fighting a losing battle. Already he was being blown further and further off course.

With a burst of strength he struggled harder, the furious buzzing of his wings lost in the shriek of wind. Snow blew into his face, blinding him. Within his small beetle body, Ringo's heart was sinking fast. Sam had been right, he was never going to make it. Soon, he realised, his wings would ice up and his muscles would fail. Then he would be swept out to sea on the gale, never to be heard of again.

Out to sea.

A thought sparked in Ringo's tiny but much-more-intelligent-than-the-average-beetle's brain. He might not be able to fly *against* the wind, but what if he let it *blow* him instead? Far across the Atlantic Ocean, Sam's broom would still be where she'd left it in a clearing in the woods in the ghost town of Sawyer Bottom. And Sam's broom could fly through *anything*.

With the thought of Sam, Ringo clicked his pincers together with fresh determination. He couldn't fail her. He couldn't let her become evil. He had to bring help, so that she could defeat Diabolica. The fate of the world rested on his shiny back, and *that* was going to make great reading when *Ringo: Beetle of Destiny* came out.

Ignoring the cold, Ringo turned in mid-air. The hurricane caught beneath his outstretched wings, throwing him through the tempest like a very small supersonic jet. Peering down, he watched the ground speed past through gaps in the snow storm and his heart lifted once more. Ahead of him was the Atlantic Ocean, and across the ocean was Sam's broom.

Very very quietly, Ringo said "wheeeeee."

7
Who's Bad?

Swaying a little on heels that were far too high for a young girl, Sam *click-click-clicked* her way past tall candlesticks and portraits of Diabolica towards the throne of the Most High and Superior Wicked Witch. Where her feet clattered, frogs hurriedly hopped out of her way. Behind her trailed the hem of a flowing black dress; an elegant off-the-shoulder number made from bat fur and spider lace. In the candlelight, her freshly washed hair sparkled with gems of poison green that matched the wickedness that sparkled in her eyes.

"Good evening mother, I have come to apologise," she said, her voice echoing from the distant walls and carved ceiling above. She dropped an only-very-slightly-clumsy curtsey before the throne. "And to tell you that from now I will be a daughter you can be proud of. An evil daughter."

Diabolica Nightshade stopped stroking the fluffy white kitten in her lap and stared at Sam in amazement.

She wasn't an easy person to surprise but, for once, she was completely and utterly gobsmacked. "Eh?" she managed to squeak.

"I've been thinking about what you said," Sam continued. "And you're right. Being good was boring, so now I'm going to be nasty instead." She twirled, showing off her dress. Light scattered off jewels. "What do you think?"

Lifting the kitten to her face, Diabolica rubbed its nose against her own and said, "I don't know. What do we think Mr Popsy?"

Mr Popsy said nothing. Kittens are like that. Instead, he batted her chin with one sweet little paw. Settling him back into her lap, Diabolica returned her attention to Sam. "Well," she said. "Mr Popsy and I think that this is another one of your silly plot-foiling plans. We think you're fibbing."

"But mother…" Sam protested.

Diabolica waved a hand to silence her. "We think you're trying to fool us into believing you're on our side and then – when we least expect it – you'll betray us." She paused for a moment, and added, "Does that sound about right? Mummy's not *completely* stupid you know."

Sam's eyes glowed green in the flickering light, "You're right not to trust me," she said. "I've been a *terrible* daughter. But I really do want to be a proper wicked witch now. You know, dabbling in the dark arts, taking over the world, blowing up gerbils: stuff like that. Please believe me mother. I want to be just like you."

"Hmmm," hmmmed Diabolica. "For some reason I can't help thinking of the words 'pants on fire'."

"You think I'm lying," said Sam quietly. "Then give me a truth potion."

For the second time that evening Diabolica was flummoxed with surprise. Blinking, she said, "W-well yes. Yes. I suppose that *would* work. Umm, very well, a truth potion it is." Clicking her fingers, she shouted to a zombie witch who was standing by the doors, groaning "Di-a-bol-i-ca" and trying to eat her own hair. "You. Yes *you,* revolting shuffly thing. Take that wig out of your mouth and go to my potion cabinet. Bring me the truth potion. Second shelf down, behind the poorly stomach potion."

"Have you got a poorly stomach?" Sam asked her mother as the zombie-witch shuffled away.

"Oh it's not a *medicine,*" replied Diabolica. "It *gives* people a poorly stomach. When I'm bored I give it the zombies and watch them trying to shuffle to the toilet in time."

"Hilarious," chuckled Sam. "You're a genius mother."

"Well yes. Yes I am. Thank you. Not everyone notices that you know." Despite herself, Diabolica found that she was rather liking her new and improved daughter. She shook her head and reminded herself that Sam was almost certainly trying to pull so much wool over her eyes that she might as well be wearing a sheep on her face.

"Di-a-bol-i-ca. Po-tion." The zombie witch returned holding a small bottle in its hands.

Tiny rainbows appeared in the air when Diabolica pulled the cork. "I saved this from the Most Superior High and Wicked Witch Trials after Igor or Helza or whatever you call her tricked Esmelia into making it," she said. "Say what you like about Igor but she does make a sensational potion. A couple of drops should be more than enough to find out whether you're telling mummy whoppers or not."

Carefully, Sam took the bottle from Diabolica's hand.

Tipping her head back, she poured the entire contents into her mouth and handed Diabolica the empty bottle.

She swallowed.

For a moment, nothing happened. Then, before Sam could stop herself, she blurted out, "I once didn't change my vest for a week." Horrified, she slapped her hands over her mouth.

With a faint smile, Diabolica lounged back in her throne and ran a hand over Mr Popsy's thick fur. *"Excellent,"* she said. "This is going to be *such* fun. Why don't you sit down my dear."

Sam pulled a stool forward and sat at Diabolica's feet, arranging her dress carefully. In doing so, she took her hands from her mouth, leaving it free to say, "And I used to flick bogies in Esmelia's dinner."

"That was kind of you. Esmelia would have liked that. But enough of this chit-chat. Tell me Samantha, truthfully, have you *really* decided to turn bad?"

Nodding enthusiastically, Sam replied, "Oh yes. From now on I'm going to be totally evil."

Diabolica blinked in surprise and sniffed the bottle. It was definitely truth potion. There was no way that Sam could be lying. "I see," she said slowly. "So you're definitely not planning to betray me then?"

A pained look crossed Sam's face. "Betray my own mother?" she said. "I don't think I'd want to do that."

Diabolica steepled her fingers. "And why, might I ask, have you had this change of heart?"

"Ever since I became a witch, everyone's been telling me I should be nasty – you, Lilith, Esmelia. I just realised you were all right. A witch *should* be nasty."

"Properly nasty?" asked Diabolica. "It's not just about being a little bit annoying you know. You'll have to use the dark magic if you want to be as wicked as me. What do you think of that?"

Sam's eyes widened. "The dark magic is so *powerful,*" she said with wonder in her voice. "And so *glamorous.* Ever since I used it yesterday I've wanted to do it again."

Diabolica could hardly believe her ears. "How are you doing this?" she hissed suddenly. "No one can lie through a truth potion."

"I'm not lying, mother," Sam replied, staring into Diabolica's eyes. "Everything I'm telling you is the simple truth."

Diabolica's heart pounded. Sam wasn't using magic – she would have been able to tell – and there was no possible way to trick the potion. The only possible explanation was that Sam *was* telling the truth. Narrowing her eyes, Diabolica decided to try a different approach. "Since I brought you here I've had a sneaky feeling that you don't really like me very much," she said. "It's the way you keep saying that you hate me I think. So, last question: what do you *really* think of me?" She tapped The Black Wand of Ohh Please Don't Turn Me Into Aaaarghh… Ribbett against her cheek, and waited, certain that Sam wouldn't be able to answer.

But Sam could answer. Reaching out, she and took Diabolica's hand. "Ever since I can remember I've wanted a mother and I couldn't have wished for one as beautiful as you," she whispered.

Choking back an unexpected sob, Diabolica looked at Sam with shining eyes. "Really?" she whispered back.

Sam nodded and squeezed her mother's hand.

Diabolica shook her head, still unable to believe that Sam wasn't somehow tricking her. There was one way of making sure, she realised. A way that would prove beyond doubt that Sam really was evil. Holding up a finger, she said, "If you really are wicked, there's something I want you to do for me."

"Anything," replied Sam. "Just name it."

"Your friend, Helza Poppin, is in the dungeons.

As luck would have it the dungeons are also full of torture devices… Do you see where I'm going with this?"

Diabolica watched Sam closely, looking for any sign of horror or hesitation. All she saw was a twinkle of evil glee in Sam's eyes.

"You want me to torture her?"

"Yes, my dear. It's just a tiny little thing, but it would mean so much to mummy. Of course, if you don't want to hurt your little friend…" Diabolica allowed her voice to trail off. Her eyes were fixed on Sam's face, expecting her to refuse at any moment.

Instead, Sam smiled. The smile grew into a grin. "Oh it's not *that,*" she said, waving her had breezily. "It's just that I've got a much much better idea."

"And what might that be?"

Sam glanced at the bald, drooling zombie-witch by the door. Its cheeks were stuffed and a small tuft of hair was sticking out between its lips. Feeling eyes watching, it mumbled "Di-a-bol-i-ca" through a mouth full of wig.

"I really want to turn her into a zombie," Sam replied. "Can I mother? Please, please, please let me turn Helza into a zombie. I promise I'll make her stick her head down the toilet and everything."

Clapping her hands together in delight, Diabolica stood. "My girl. My own dear sweet *evil* girl," she said with tearful pride. "Come to mummy."

Rising from her stool, Sam fell into Diabolica Nightshade's arms. "Oh mother," she whispered sadly as Diabolica hugged her tight. "I'm going to show you just how evil I can be."

8

Beeflemania

Dropping through white branches, Ringo landed on the forest floor. Through the trees he could see a small, half-ruined house almost invisible under a thick blanket of snow. Icicles hung in curtains from the eaves of the roof. Framed by the window and lit by the warm glow of old-fashioned oil lamps, a dumpy woman in a turban leaned over a crystal ball at a table inside. Around her plates and cups were flying onto shelves as a friendly spirit did the washing up.

Ringo hadn't come to see Blanche Nightly. Ignoring the ghost hunter, he peered through the silently falling snow until he spotted what he had come for. Leaning against a crumbling wall, next to the outside toilet, was Sam's broom; just where she'd left it.

Ringo forced his freezing legs into action and scuttled through the snow, raising a small white cloud that glittered in the moonlight. His pincers clicked with excitement as he hurried up the broomstick's frosted twigs and onto the polished handle. Beneath his feet he

71

felt it twitch. The broom recognised him. Ringo jigged a beetle dance step. Nothing could stop him now.

Stroking the polished wood gently, he thought about Esmelia and the Goblin's Elbow. He thought about Sam in danger. He thought about speed. And he thought about the chapter in *Ringo: Beetle of Destiny* which would tell of his heroic dash over the Atlantic.

The broom understood. It quivered for a moment, shook off its covering of ice like a dog shaking off water, and rose up into the air. Leaping forward, it stopped suddenly. Directly in its path stood Blanche Nightly.

The tubby ghost hunter put her hands on her hips, peered down and said "Oh, it's *you*. When the spirits said a hero was coming I expected someone a little bit bigger."

Ringo waved at her to get out of his way and urged the broom forward again. Blanche's hand shot out and gripped the wooden handle tightly before it could move. "You just wait right there Mister Beetle," she said firmly. "The spirits have spoken and they said that a hero will come to Sawyer Bottom to lead an army of witches to the Bleak Fortress. And the spirits are *never* wrong." She paused, then added, "except about those mushrooms being good to eat, and Uncle Derek having ten million dollars stuffed in an old sock, and… well… let's just say the spirits aren't *always* wrong."

In the distance, something howled. Something that made Blanche shudder. "We've tried to fight them," she said quietly. "But there are too many. Werewolves and ghouls and wraiths – wraiths are the wispy ones, aren't they? – plus demon things and slimy creatures of the dreaded whatnot. Dragons too." Looking down at Ringo, she sighed and said, "They keep coming through from the dark pits of the netherworld. It's the magic: the dark magic. It's everywhere now. Even the spirits are afraid. They keep telling me that there's worse things coming and even being dead is no escape. We have to stop Diabolica, but she has the Bleak Fortress well guarded. Small as you are, you might be the world's last hope."

The world's last hope stood on his spindly back legs. If his chest could have swelled with pride it would have done. Unfortunately, beetle chests aren't built for swelling with pride. Instead, he struck a heroic pose.

"Well, I suppose what you lack in size you make up for in courage," said Blanche.

From above came a crash of breaking twigs and the cackling of witches. "Look, look, I'm *famous!*" screeched Enid waving a newspaper. "It's me, I'm the very very ugly old lady I am."

Snatching the paper from her hand, Blanche looked at the headline: "WITCH WINTER?"

Beneath it was a blurred photo, taken in heavy snow. It showed a black blob wearing a pointy hat kicking another black blob that looked a bit like a large dog if you squinted.

Blanche's eyes flicked over the story.

The weather is out of control. Wolves howl in the night. Strange wispy figures flit through our streets. So far, no-one has been able to explain these events. Now, one man has taken a photo that, he believes, proves that witches are involved.

Said Mr Mark Trolley: "I was trying to dig my car out of the snow near Stonehenge when the wolf jumped me. I've never been so scared in my life. It had great big teeth with drool dripping off them. Exactly the sort of teeth that are all the better to eat you with. It was just about to rip my face off when there was this horrible screeching noise. Then an old lady fell out of the sky and whopped it right in the face with a frying pan. I could tell she was a witch straight away because she was sitting on one of those old-fashioned broomsticks. Plus she had a pointy hat. Oh, and she was very very ugly. Yes, I know it's not a very good photo but it really was a witch."

With weather men and scientists still baffled by the bizarre weather, Mr Trolley believes it is supernatural. "It stands to reason that it's all down to witches. Everyone knows they like endless winter. You never see a witch in a bikini do you?"

Jim Salmon, TV's weather man, responded, "There is no reason to think that the strange winter is due to witchcraft. Magic doesn't really exist you see. Really."

Blanche lowered the newspaper. "You're supposed to stay out of sight," she snapped. "People won't be too happy if they find out what's *really* going on. We don't want them to start burning witches again, do we?"

"I dunno luvvie," said Dot. "I'm freezing."

"Ooo you're right Dot. It'd be lovely putting our feet up by a nice warm fire. And witches burn really well. They can use Foul Betty if they likes," she added jabbing a thumb over her shoulder. "She won't mind."

"That's right," grinned Foul Betty screwing her face up even more than it was already screwed up. "I'm made out of wood."

Seeing Ringo drumming his feet against the broomstick handle impatiently, Blanche coughed. "Anyway," she said. "The reason I called you all back…"

"Where's this hero you was gabbling about then?"

interrupted Enid, looking around. "I don't see no heroes."

"Ooo yes. Where's this big strapping hero with shiny muscles?" chuckled Dot. "I loves big shiny muscly heroes. On toast."

"Has he got a mysterious sword and a birthmark?" shouted Ridikula Staffonly from the back. "He ain't a proper hero unless he's got a mysterious sword and a birthmark."

Blanche coughed again, and pointed at Ringo.

A mass of bent and wobbly old witches leaned forward, squinting through the falling snow at Sam's broom.

"Is that it," screeched Enid. "A beetle? You spoiled my werewolf kicking and dragged us halfway around the world to look at a *beetle?*"

"It's not just any old beetle, it's Sam's familiar," said Blanche.

"I don't care if it's Cakula von Drakula's best friend Gerald," shrieked Enid. "It's a flippin' *beetle.*"

"I ain't following a beetle into battle. It's not right. People would laugh."

"But the spirits said…"

"Pah. What do spirits know?" sneered Enid. "If they're so flippin' clever, how come they're all *dead?*"

Blanche had had enough. "Shut up the lot of you!"

she bellowed. "No-one is saying we've got to follow him into *battle*. We've just got to *follow* him. He's going to get us into the Bleak Fortress. He's not actually going to fight."

Ringo crossed his arms huffily. He'd been looking forward to fighting.

"Weeeeell," said Enid after a while. "I suppose if he's only showing us the way, that wouldn't be too bad. What do you say Dot my pumpkin?"

"Meh, s'pose so," Dot grumbled.

"Dot says it's alright," said Enid. "Alright then beetle, you can get us into the Bleak Fortress. Better not get in my way when the fighting starts though," she finished, slapping a dented frying pan on the palm of her hand with a dull *clooiiiing*.

After only a quick break for a nice cup of tea and a biscuit, a small army of old and, in many cases, completely mad, witches rose through the bare branches of the forest. Fanning out into a "V" formation, they streaked into the storm like ragged black shooting stars. At the tip of the "V", Ringo stood proud on Sam's broom. He had an army. He was going to save the world. It had been foretold by the spirits.

And even more importantly than saving the world, he was going to save Sam.

9
Spine-Chilling Sinisterness

Face smeared with dirt and straw sticking out of her hair, Helza Poppin was dragged through the doors of the Great Throne Room. Struggling in the grip of two zombie witches, she looked up and saw Sam. At once, her face brightened. "Hi," she croaked. "What's with the frock? It's *so* not you."

"You don't like it?" said Sam, twirling. "It was very expensive, but then hand-peeled lizard skin always is." She winked at her friend and leaned over to stir a small cauldron at her feet with the wand Esmelia had given her months before in Pigsnout Wood.

As Sam bent, Helza caught sight of Diabolica behind her, lounging in her throne with Mr Popsy on her lap. The power-crazed-evil-sorceress-out-to-take-over-the-world waved and returned her attention to playing with the kitten.

Helza looked from Sam to Diabolica and back again, confusion on her face. Sam smiled and carried on stirring as her friend was hauled across the floor, feet dragging on the cold stone. The wand she was using was just a stick with some surprisingly good carving, but it was doing the trick. She screwed her eyes closed and let dark magic flow along its length and down into the black liquid. Foul-smelling black smoke trickled over the cauldron's rim. Magic coiled in its bubbling depths.

"So, wassup bud?" said Helza as the zombie-witches hauled her upright a few feet from Sam. "What's with the whole dragging people out of their dungeon thing?"

Sam didn't answer. Instead, she nudged a frog off the seat of a small throne that had been found in one of the Bleak Fortress's hundreds of forgotten rooms, dusted down and placed next to Diabolica's. Once used by Squat Wee Maureen (Most High and Superior Wicked Witch 1095–1111), it was just the right size for her. Making herself comfortable, she tapped her wand on her cheek and looked her friend up and down.

"What's going on here?" said Helza, staring at her friend. "You look, like, totally different." She glared at Diabolica and spat, "What have you done to her?"

"Oh, I haven't…" Diabolica began.

She stopped when Sam put her hand up and said

softly, "Please mother. I want to do this alone."

Diabolica smiled and bent down to whisper into Mr Popsy's ear. Ignoring Helza's questions, Sam pointed to the cauldron with her wand. "You know what that is, don't you?" she asked.

Helza sniffed the air. "I smell Pizen Sickberry, Brainwort, Deathly Creeper, Coffinwood, the juice of a freshly squeezed mole and newts' eyes." She closed her eyes while she added the ingredients together in her head. They blinked open again with a look of shock. "Which means it's a zombification potion."

"You're right, of course, it's a zombification potion," said Sam, nodding. "And I made it especially for you... *Igor.*"

Beneath the dirt, Helza's face went white. *"You* made it?" she said. "For *me?* I thought we were friends."

Sam glanced at Diabolica and then back at Helza. "I have my mother now," she said. "She is all the friend I need. And I was getting tired of you anyway. Even the way you talk is, like, *sooo* totally annoying." Rising from her throne, Sam walked around Helza, the train of her lizardy dress swishing on the stone floor. Feeling that the time was just about right for it, she laughed, "Mwah ha ha HA HA."

Silence.

"Oh, I see," Helza said quietly. "You've gone evil, like your barmy mom. Explains the dress and the funny little throne I guess."

Nodding, Sam leaned towards her and hissed, "That's right, I'm evil now. And you know what, *bud?* It's *waaay* more fun."

As Sam's face pressed close to her own, Helza whispered urgently, "This is a trick, right? You're just pretending."

"Sowwy Igor," said Sam, sticking out her bottom lip and pulling a sad face. "It's not a twick, or a silly plot, or anything like that." Dipping a hand into Helza's pocket, she pulled out a small bottle. Tossing it up in the air, she caught it and slipped it down the front of her dress. "And yes, I *did* remember that you have a bottle of anti-zombie potion. *You* won't be needing it though."

Helza gasped. "I-I d-don't believe it," she stammered. "You're my best friend. Doesn't that mean anything to you?"

"Bo*ring,*" Sam yawned. Stepping back, she stirred the cauldron again. Black smoke curled around her ankles. She nodded at the zombie-witches.

"No!" Helza cried, struggling afresh as she was shoved forward. "Please. Don't do this Sam. Please. I spent years with Diabolica. She's a killer. Please don't be evil. Listen to me. I'm your friend…" Her voice choked off as the two zombie-witches pushed her face into the thick smoke that was now billowing from the cauldron.

Sam watched as Helza tried to hold her breath. It was impossible. Tears glistening on her filthy face, she spluttered and coughed as she breathed in the awful smoke.

She stopped struggling.

The zombie-witches released their grip.

Helza stood. Her eyes dry, and blank like the eyes of a dead fish. Her mouth sagged open. Her arms hung at her sides, fingers curled into claws.

Turning slightly to face her new mistress, she moaned, "Saaaaaam."

"Oh well *done,* Samantha," cried Diabolica, clapping. "That was *perfect*. You're a natural. The mockery, the 'mwah ha ha', the snatching away of hope… It was all just so *evil."*

"Thank you mother," said Sam. "May I play with it now?"

"Go on then darling, enjoy yourself."

Sam prodded the Helza thing on the nose with her wand. "Hey, Igor you shuffling lame-brain thing, go stand in the corner and bang your head against the wall," she giggled.

Droning "Saaaaam" Helza shuffled through the frogs to obey.

"Lovely," crowed Diabolica. "I must say I *am* enjoying sharing these little mother and daughter moments…" She stopped for a moment, tapping The Black Wand of Ohh Please Don't Turn Me Into Aaaarghh… Ribbett against her cheek. Slowly, she continued. "In fact, you've been such a bad little girl I'm wondering whether I should crown you too. Would you like that darling? Would you like to rule the world at mummy's side?"

Sam curtsied. "After everything I've done?" she said quietly, "I don't deserve such an honour."

"Nonsense. All that goody goody silliness is over and done with now. Mummy is very proud of you."

"Well," said Sam. "If you think I might be able to help you…" She looked Diabolica in the eye. "And if it means I get some new dresses. Oh, and will I get to spread pain and misery too?"

"Just like your mother," Diabolica purred happily. "Always thinking about pretty clothes and plunging the world into a pit of horror."

Sam smiled at her mother sweetly.

"And I suppose you should have your wand back too," said Diabolica, watching Sam carefully. "Your *real* wand. Not that old twig."

Sam felt her heart begin to thump wildly. Somewhere deep within the Bleak Fortress The White Wand of… Oi You Could Have Someone's Eye Out With That flared with sudden power. With a twinkle of evil in her eye, Sam shrugged and said, "I'd almost forgotten about that old thing. I suppose it might come in handy, but white's not really my colour."

10

Esmelia (Finally) Hatches a Plan

Lionel Ulcer goggled at the kitchen of the Goblin's Elbow and pulled out the remains of his hair. The floor was littered with pots and pans and broken crockery, and swimming in an ankle deep lake of soup. Food was running down the walls, bats swooped around the ceiling, and the chef was crying in the corner. He hadn't seen anything like it since his wife's sister had last come to visit. "Madam," the landlord gibbered. "We are supposed to serve dinner in ten minutes."

A besplattered and dripping Esmelia stopped stirring and glared up from a saucepan that bubbled slime over the cooker. The brim of her hat flopped down over her eyes. Pushing her hat back, and wiping gravy from her forehead, she said, *"Some* of us are trying to hatch a plot here, if you don't mind, thankyousovery much. Prob'ly tryin' to save the world and suchlike."

"But… but you've been at it since *yesterday.* Perhaps it's time to give up?"

Esmelia scowled and grabbed something to threaten the landlord with. "You watch it," she hissed. "I could have your eye out with this…" she looked down, "… with this chocolate éclair."

Peering out from behind Professor Dentrifice's robe, Wolfbang Pigsibling snorted with barely contained laughter.

"Shhhh," shushed the professor. "She'll hear you."

"All she's come up with so far is a recipe for leek and washing-up liquid surprise," Wolfbang Pigsibling said under his breath. "She's *rubbish.*"

"Eh?" hissed Esmelia, turning her glare upon the apprentice. "What's that you said?"

"Oh dear, you've done it now," said Professor Dentrifice, taking a step backwards, carefully putting himself out of range of Esmelia's creamy chocolate pastry.

Caught in Esmelia's glare once more, Wolfbang Pigsibling's face turned green. Then red. "I said you're *rubbish,*" he blurted. "And a bully. I'm sick of it. You can't do magic and couldn't plot your way out of a wet paper bag. All you can do is cackle like a cement mixer."

For the tiniest of tiny seconds, Esmelia was speechless. Not only was she too shocked to talk but there was an unpleasant hollow feeling in her stomach.

The little wizard sounded exactly like her own apprentice. It was almost as if Sam was in the kitchen, moaning as usual.

The tiniest of seconds was soon over. Esmelia took a step towards Wolfbang Pigsibling. "I'll show *you* magic," she hissed. "The magic of a broken arm. Followed by the magic of a punch in the earhole."

The trembling apprentice squeaked, "You don't frighten me. I can do fireballs. What can *you* do?"

"I can do *you* a mischief for a start," said Esmelia, rolling her sleeves back.

"Oh dear oh dear oh dear," murmured Professor Dentrifice, trying to stand at the back of a gaggle of wizards who, at exactly the same time, were all trying to stand behind him. "Now then, now then, let's not have any unpleasantness."

Esmelia Sniff and Wolfbang Pigsibling both ignored him. "I don't believe you're even a proper witch," whimpered the apprentice. "That *frog* would make a better witch than you." Without taking his eyes off Esmelia's he pointed at Cakula von Drakula, who was sitting on an upturned saucepan in the middle of the floor.

Cakula shrugged. It was true.

"You disgustin' little weasel," Esmelia hissed, looming over the boy. "I'll have you know I'm Acting Most Superior High and Wicked Witch, I am. It said so in *The Cackler*. All I have to do is click my fingers, like this…" she clicked her fingers under the boy's nose, "…and every witch in the world'll come running."

"If you're s-so powerful w-where are they then?"
Wolfbang Pigsibling stuttered.

Every window shattered.

Snow and wind and broken glass and a small army
of shrieking witches blasted into the kitchen.
In a whirlwind of black rags and warts and raggedy hair
they circled among the rafters, cackling and shrieking.

Esmelia blinked at her own fingers and then glared at the apprentice wizard. "See," she spat.

Wolfbang Pigsibling worked his jaw up and down, but no sound came out. His eyes looked like they might actually pop out of their sockets on stalks at any second, Esmelia noticed. She hoped so. It was something she'd always wanted to see.

"I'd better just go and... er... be somewhere that's not here," he gargled.

"That's a good boy," Esmelia said kindly, patting him on the head. As he hurried away, her heavy boot lashed out and caught the seat of his wizarding robe. "Ooops, foot slipped in all this gunk," she muttered.

As the apprentice staggered through the door, Esmelia straightened up and folded her arms. Forty-one broomsticks pointed towards her. Forty witches, with snowdrifts piled up on the brims of their hats and icicles dripping from their noses, squinted through the steam and smoke. Behind them, Lionel Ulcer was busy doing sums on a flapping scrap of paper. Huddled together, the wizards nudged each other and tidied their beards, eying the new arrivals and whispering things like, "Cor, look at the warts on *her,*" and "Phwoaarrr."

One broom drifted forward and stopped in front of Esmelia's stony face, its only rider a small beetle. Scratched into the handle were the words "This broom belongs to Sam." As the old witch watched, the writing wriggled and changed. Now, it said, "This broom is on loan to Esmelia."

Esmelia wasn't the sort of person who usually smiled unless someone was getting hurt. Smiling made her face ache and gave people the idea that she might, possibly, have a sense of humour. But now the corners of her mouth twitched. She rubbed her hands together in glee. "Esmelia Sniff," she murmured to herself. "You *shall* go to the Bleak Fortress." Winking at Ringo, she said "Wotcha you nasty little insect."

"Why've we stopped here?" interrupted a witch wearing thick goggles. "I thought we was going to Transylvania. Is it a toilet break? Only I went five minutes ago."

"But we was still in the air five minutes ago."

"I know."

A witch called Agnes Punishment leaned forward over the handle of her broomstick, peering closely at Esmelia. "Is that young Stinky Sniff?" she said. "What's the beetle brought us to see *her* for? She's a cretin.

Famous for it."

Esmelia scowled. "Oi," she said. "I *am* the Acting Most Superior High and Wicked…"

"She ain't bad at knocking teeth in though. You have to give her that," crowed Dot. "She might be total disgrace to witchcraft, but she's got a lovely left hook."

"… Witch." Esmelia realised she may as well pick her nose for all the notice the other witches were taking of her, so she picked her nose. And while she picked her gaze rested on the befrogginated Cakula von Drakula.

Somewhere in the twisty dark depths of Esmelia's mind a light flashed on at last. A light that said "Hello Devious Plan!!" As plots went, it was, indeed, a winner. As usual, it ended with Esmelia being Most Superior High and Wicked Witch. *And that,* she told herself, *is what plots is all about.*

Esmelia bent and grabbed Cakula round the throat while the other witches jibber-jabbered around her.

"Ooo yes, she give that Deadly Nightshade a great poke in the eye. It was a pleasure to watch was that poke."

"Is she going to eat that chocolate éclair? I'm starving."

"I *hates* that Stinky Sniff though."

"Oh, we all *hates* her but she *does* know her way around a plot, even if she is the worst witch since someone put a pointy hat on a duck. I'll bet you a bucket of earwax she's hatched up some sneaky and devious way to get us into the Bleak Fortress."

"The spirits said the beetle would show us the way, and he's led us here, so Esmelia *must* have a plan to get us in," said Blanche Nightly firmly.

There was a cough behind the witches. Forty heads snapped round to glare at Professor Dentrifice. "Dear ladies," he said. "Dear *lovely* ladies. Sweet, beautiful, ladies... I'm afraid there must be some mistake. Esmelia's tried her best, of course she has, but no plots have been hatched here..."

"Who gave you permission to talk?" said Esmelia. "And who said I ain't got a plot?"

Silence fell. The wizard stared around the wreckage of the kitchen. "But..."

Lifting Cakula up to her face, Esmelia said slowly, "We'd never all of us get into the Bleak Fortress without being spotted. But one witch... One witch on her own. Well, *one witch* might make it. Especially if she was the sneaky and devious kind of witch."

"Well you're not leaving *me* here," said Blanche firmly.

"Nor me."

"Me neither."

"No, you can't leave them *here*," gabbled Lionel Ulcer who had already decided to put a sign on the door saying "Strictly No Witches."

"Oh, you'll all be coming alright," cackled Esmelia, dropping Cakula into the palm of her hand and lifting her up for all to see. "But only *one witch* is going to the Bleak Fortress."

The witches glanced at each other as they tried to puzzle out Esmelia's riddle. "What's she talking about Enid?" said Dot.

"She's talking mad Dot," said Enid.

"I ain't mad," continued Esmelia, tossing Cakula gently up and down in front of the witches' eyes. She sighed. Sometimes witches could be very stupid indeed. "Let me put it this way," she said quietly, holding up Cakula again. "Who's got a good befroggination spell?"

The witches looked at each other. "Err, we *all* has. We're *witches* dearie," said Dot.

11
The Secret Library

Sam strode quickly along a corridor in an old part of the
Bleak Fortress, her way illuminated only by the silver
light of a waxing moon flooding in shafts through dusty
windows. The Midwinter Moon had almost arrived.
The storm had finally blown itself out. Beyond
the Bleak Fortress, the Transylvanian
mountains glittered.

An unearthly shriek rattled
the windows. She stopped for
a moment and looked up
as the moon was blotted
out. The sleek shape of
a dragon soared across
the landscape on bat-
like leathery wings, its
neck stretched and its
head lifted to spout
hateful fire. It was
beautiful, wicked, and it

had come to serve Diabolica.

Sam shivered and carried on walking, heels clicking softly through dust.

Elsewhere, the castle had changed. Cold corridors that had echoed only with the dragging of zombie-witch feet were teeming with the undead and monstrous creatures of the dreadful pits. The air was thick with the stench of the tomb and the whispers of shades and spooks. Claws scraped on the stone floors. The Bleak Fortress was full, but hideous fiends were still arriving to swell Diabolica's army of evil.

The part of the castle where Sam was walking was empty though. None of the undead were big readers. It had taken days to find and Sam guessed that not even Diabolica knew where it was. Glancing over her shoulder, she said "Please try and keep up." The shuffling thing that was Helza Poppin shuffled a little faster. Rounding a corner, Sam saw what she had come for. A large door with a heavily cobwebbed sign that said "Library", and – underneath, in slightly smaller letters – "Silence Please: Strictly No Screaming."

Sam pushed the door. It was stuck. Putting her shoulder against the wood, she heaved. Slowly, it inched open, pushing against a deep layer of dust. Silently, Sam waved Helza forward. The castle's newest zombie-witch held out a candle-topped skull on which wax had dribbled, making the skull look exactly like it was wearing a white wig.

A match flared. Sam lit the candle and peered around the door.

A few feet away, a skeleton in a pointed hat was slumped over a desk. The librarian had died at her post with her head in a book. Tip-toeing past the dead witch, Sam glanced down. Curious to see what story had been so good that the librarian had forgotten to carry on living, Sam read a few of the upside-down lines: *"Oh Ratface, my own darling witch,"* sighed Ravencourt Nightwalker, *his manly wizard beard rippling with desire. "I want to take your nose in my arms and kiss every one of your sweet warts…"*

It was not the sort of book Sam had come for. She held her candle skull aloft and looked around.

And gasped.

Stretching into darkness above were walls of books. More books than she had ever seen before. Books that contained all the knowledge of five thousand years of witchcraft. Shelf upon shelf upon shelf of them. Helza trailing behind, Sam scurried through the dust to the nearest and held the candle close to a row of battered

leather spines. Blowing away cobwebs and running a finger along them, her lips moved as she read: *Coven Ready: A History of Witchcraft in Eighteen Extremely Boring Volumes by Drysa Prune; The Godmother; Adventures With Owls...* Here was treasure that Sam had never expected to find. Books she could spend her entire life reading. But none of them would do. She shook her head, and whispered, "Bring me that ladder" over her shoulder.

Obediently, Helza pushed a tall stepladder across the floor. Sam climbed it eagerly, her eyes already searching out the titles on the next row of books: *The Properties and Uses of Newts' Eyeballs.* No. *The Toad Whisperer.* No.

An hour passed, and then another. Slowly, the candle burned down as Sam looked at book after book in the gloomy library. Occasionally she would pull one from the shelf and leaf through dry pages covered with sinister drawings and spider droppings before jamming it back onto the shelf with a snort of disappointment. Only a tiny flickering stub was left by the time she found what she was looking for. On a high shelf at the end of a row was a thick book called *Plans and Drawings for the Castle of The Most Superior High and Wickedest Witch*

(The Bleak Fortress) including Secret Passages, Pits, Traps and Very Many Dungeons by Gruselda the Skanky. Holding her breath, Sam opened it, dislodging centuries of dust that dropped onto Helza's head in a small puff. Her eyes scanned down a page. It showed hundreds of passages running through the castle, with entrances through hidden doors. At the bottom someone had scrawled in different handwriting, "Load of old rubbish. Why ain't there any rippling wizards?"

This was the book she had come for.

Sam closed the book and tucked it under her arm. She was just about to clamber down the ladder when another caught her eye. *Magical Principals: A Study of The Universal Laws of Magic* by Mistress Isa Newt, Witch. Pulling it from the shelf, she opened it curiously. Isa Newt's handwriting was small and difficult to read but Sam managed to make out the words by the light of the dying candle.

… For magical force binds our planet together, balancing good against evil as summer balances winter. This same force holds among all the stars and planets of the universe…

Turning the page, she read another section.

… If the balance is tipped too far eventually the universe will freeze over. All light will die and the darkness of the netherworlds shall rule forever. See diagram a…

Sam frowned. The pages were covered in difficult-looking drawings and thick with words she didn't recognise, but something told her that Isa Newt's book was important. She tucked it under her arm with the other. And then, because she couldn't help herself, she also took a book called *A Wizard's Passion* and added it to the pile. Not bothering to check the books out, she hurried away, Helza shuffling behind her.

12

Sergeant Sniff's Amphibious Army

As Acting Most Superior High and Wicked Witch, Esmelia had insisted on taking charge of the small army of witches. While the army hadn't been very happy about this it had quickly agreed among itself that there wasn't very much it *was* happy about and, anyway, *someone* had to take the lead. As that person was likely to be the first one Diabolica would turn into a small pile of stoat droppings, they had also agreed that it might as well be Stinky Sniff. Having decided that Esmelia would be allowed to lead, at least for as long as she was still person-shaped, forty grumbling witches lined up in front of her in the snow outside the Goblin's Elbow.

The power of leadership had gone to Esmelia's head, just a little bit. Marching up and down before the small witch army, scrawny chest puffed out and Sam's broom tucked under her arm, she bellowed, "Right then, you 'orrible lot, stand to atten-SHUN!"

"Eh, speak up dearie," said a witch at the back, cupping a hand to her ear.

"SHUT UP Corporal Punishment. I'm doing the talking here."

The small army muttered themselves into silence. "Right, listen up you bunch of big girls' blouses, this is the plan," Esmelia roared. "First everyone gets befrogginated then I smuggles you into the Bleak Fortress in me knickers. Soon as whatserface – Dribbly Nightowl – crowns herself, I clicks me fingers, everyone changes back and hits her with a binding spell, then I'll grab The Black Wand of Ohh Please Don't Turn Me Into Aaaarghh… Ribbett." Rubbing her hands together, she added under her breath, "And when I've got The Black Wand of Ohh Please Don't Turn Me Into Aaaarghh… Ribbett there won't be no more of this 'Acting' Most Superior High and Wicked Witch nonsense."

"Errr… Excuse me," said a witch near the back.

"What do you want Private Staffonly?"

"Did you say you were going to smuggle us into the Bleak Fortress in your *knickers?*"

"That's right."

"Only, at my age, I don't think I wants to go

anywhere in your knickers dearie."

"She's got a point there, she has," said Dot. "I'd rather eat me own knees than go flyin' about in Stinky Sniff's drawers."

"Why can't she carry us in a sack then?"

"*Pah,* just goes to show why I'm the brains of the operation, don't it?" sneered Esmelia. "If I gets caught, what's the first thing whatserface is going to say, eh? 'What you got in that there sack Esmelia Sniff?' That's what she'll say."

"That's true," Blanche cut in. "Even Diabolica wouldn't check for an army of frogs in Esmelia's underwear."

"That's settled then," crowed Esmelia. "Now, once I've got The Black Wand of Ohh Please Don't Turn Me Into Aaaarghh… Ribbett, what are you lot going to do?"

At once, the witches straightened up. They had been practicing all night. "Aaaand… one two three forward," they chanted together, taking a step forward. Forty boots crunched in the snow.

"One two three… *present* fingers." Forty fingers pointed at the sky.

"One two three… *lunge and poke.*" As one, the witches jabbed their fingers forward.

"I ain't saying it's perfect," said Esmelia when the witches had finished. "There's some very sloppy poking going on there. But it should give old Direbonkers a couple of black eyes she won't be forgetting in a hurry. Right then, which one of you crones is doing the spell?"

Pointy hats huddled together in the snow as the witches argued about which spell to use and who was going to perform it. Some preferred Gamma Spodley's Patent Frogulizor, others Ringworm Weaselvomit's Webfoot Wowser, and a few were keen on Wicked Stepmother's Prince Charming Special. For witches, it was a fairly polite conversation with only a few punches thrown and, before long, the cluster broke up.

Spitting a broken tooth into the snow, Enid stood to attention and said, "I'm doing it." She shot a black look over her shoulder and continued, "And I shall be using a good, old-fashioned, Croaking Curse what I made up last Thursday."

Muttering about how their own spells were much much better and who did Enid think she was, the crones and hags formed a circle. At the centre, Enid pulled a wand from her sleeve and began to chant.

Something, something, oh what was it?
Something about lurking in bogs.
Forgotten the words... err...
I think it's about cheese this bit.
And I'll just make this line up a well.
Then wave yer wand about like this.
And agrammajammy, ta da – bunch of FROGS!

Esmelia's jaw dropped open. She'd seen some terrible, truly awful, magic in her time as a witch – most of it in her own cottage – but this was beyond bad. "What was *that?*" she yelled. "A flippin' *wizard* could do better than that."

Flashes of purple light began sparkling in the air. A breeze blew up, which turned into a gentle whirlwind flashing with ribbons of dark colour.

"What was that you was saying dearie?" said Enid. And then she was gone. The sparkles faded away. Sat in a circle were forty frogs.

"Hmph," harrumphed Esmelia. "Well, come on then. One two, one two, on the double... *forward.*"

The frogs hopped towards her. "Heh heh heh," snickered Esmelia. "Now, that's what I *calls* frog marching." Scooping the first one to arrive up, she pulled her skirt up to the knee and pushed the witch-frog up the leg of her long knickers. "Oooo," she said as it squirmed around.

She reached for the frog that had been Dot a few moments before and shoved her in headfirst, too. The next hopped up, looking rather sick at the sight of Esmelia's underwear.

While the old witch was busy, another frog crept out from behind a plant pot and joined the queue. As Esmelia had once noticed, one frog looks very much like another. The new frog was quickly slipped into her knickers along with the rest.

Cakula von Drakula was going home.

Soon Esmelia's underwear was stuffed to bursting. Standing straight, she took a step. "Oooo," she said as the movement set the frogs a-squirming. Taking another, she stopped and hoisted her skirt up. "Oi, no fighting down there!" she hissed. On bandy legs, and squeaking "Goodness gracious," to herself Esmelia managed to climb aboard the broom, just as the door of the Goblin's Elbow crashed open.

"Esmelia my sweet darling," boomed Sebastian Dentrifice. "I was worried about you." He looked from her to the broom quickly. "Going somewhere?"

From beneath Esmelia's skirts one of the witches croaked loudly, a deep and long *riiiibbbettt*. The wizard glanced down. Choking, he took a hurried step backwards.

"Bleak Fortress," snapped Esmelia. "So get out of the way. And I ain't your sweet darling."

The witch-frog croaked again. This time it set off one of its neighbours. And then another. *Riiibett, riiibett, riiibettt,* croaked Esmelia's knickers.

"Gah," coughed the professor. "Ummm… that is, you can't go saving the world without me, I mean, erm… us, wizards."

"What's it got to do with *you?* This is *witch* business," snapped Esmelia as the broom began to rise and twisted around to face south. This set off a storm of protest as the frogs were thrown about. Soon, the croaking was earsplitting.

Clutching at the broom's twigs from below, Professor Dentrifice blurted out, "b-but you can't go anywhere. You're obviously very ill. Was it something you ate?"

The croaking became even louder as Esmelia settled her backside carefully on Sam's broom. "Eh?" she shouted over the noise. "What *are* you talking about you useless little man?"

A particularly loud croak from beneath Esmelia's skirt made the wizard clutch at his beard. "Your little problem," he managed to squeak, pointing to Esmelia's backside. "You know. Down there."

"It's not a problem," said Esmelia primly. "It felt a bit funny at first but its alright once you get used to it."

The broom swept forward and up. Leaving Professor Dentrifice goggling, Esmelia hurtled into the sky. "Wizards," she muttered to herself. "You'd think he'd never seen a witch with her knickers stuffed with frogs before."

And with that, she hunched over the wooden handle. "Transylvania," she said. "As fast as you like."

13
Welcome to the Bleak Fortress

The doors of the Great Throne Room groaned open. A foul smell rolled across the room. Silently, a ghoul drifted towards the throne and kneeled before Diabolica. "Misstresss, we have arrived. The time off sssufferring isss here at lassssst."

"Well, yes it is," snapped Diabolica drumming her fingernails on the arm of the throne. "My coronation is tomorrow night in fact. And you're very nearly late."

"There were witchessss waiting for ussss," hissed the ghoul, its voice dripping with spite. "Many of ussss died."

"What!" shouted Diabolica. "How could they kill that which does not live?"

The ghoul's skeleton fingers curled into fists. "They had frying panssss," it whispered. "And big bootssss."

Diabolica rolled her eyes. "You are supposed to be an army of evil spreading pain and suffering across the world. Getting trampled on by a bunch of rickety old crones with kitchen equipment isn't a very good start, is it?"

111

"We are sssorry mistressss. We ssshall make the witchessss pay."

Clutching a fur robe around herself, Sam walked slowly along the battlements of the Bleak Fortress. Free of the stench of undead beasts, she took great lungfuls of freezing fresh air. Her breath steamed, clinging to her hair and instantly forming tiny diamonds of ice. She stopped, leaned on the crumbling stone and looked out. Nothing moved in the valley below. The skies were empty. "Where *is* she?" she whispered to herself.

"Saaaaaam?" droned a voice behind her.

Glancing over her shoulder at the zombie-Helza, Sam said, "Oh, nothing. Nothing for you to worry your empty head about."

"Saaaaam."

"Shhh Helza." Raising her eyes, Sam gazed out into the night, letting her shoulders relax and allowing her mind to wander. Her breathing became deeper and slower.

For those who could see, the world was brimming with magic. Sam's wandering mind reached out into it. The darkness whispered to her. Making promises. But there was magic beyond it. Magic that only Isa Newt had ever bothered to think about. Sam reached for the same magic she had used to create The White Wand of… Oi You Could Have Someone's Eye Out With That. As she did so the words of a letter she had found in an old witch's grave came back to her. Penny Dreadful had written…

The fate o' the werld be in yer hands, an ye be all what stands 'agin the Deadly Nightshade. It be up to ye, but afore ye goes changin' the futcher ye think careful now. If'n ye wanted it, ye'd be Queen o' the Werld, an a witch queen might'n not be so bad, eh?

Sam's mind lurched with excitement as she touched the magic of the universe. It was a thousand, a million, times greater than the darkness swirling about the Earth. Again, she had the rather excellent feeling that the whole of space and time was revolving around her. But even as she touched it, the vast magic slipped away from her. It was too great to be held. Using that magic would be like trying to sew a handkerchief using a space rocket as a needle.

"Saaaaam."

The magic slipped away as a movement caught the corner of her eye. Sam's head snapped round.

There.

Sweeping low over the mountains was a speck of blackness just visible by the light of the moon. It was travelling faster than any bird, and faster than any broomstick. Any broomstick but one.

"A *last*. Something wicked this way comes," Sam whispered to herself. "Well, something annoying and smelly this way comes," she corrected herself. Taking her elbows from the cold grey stone, Sam stood straight. "Come on," she said to Helza. "Let's go and welcome Esmelia to the Bleak Fortress."

"Waaaah," wailed Esmelia Sniff to herself, holding onto her hat and clinging to the wooden handle as Sam's broom flashed across Transylvania. As a witch, riding broomsticks was nothing new to her but this one was faster than any she'd ever used. It was also staying low to avoid being seen and Esmelia's knees kept scraping on mountaintops. She suspected the broom was doing this on purpose and she was absolutely correct: it was.

Behind her, sitting on the twigs, Tiddles lashed at passing eagles with a paw. In front of her, shielding his eyes with one leg, Ringo peered into the distance. Far ahead, blazing with lights, its snow-covered turrets glinting in the moonlight, was the menacing hulk of the Bleak Fortress.

As she came closer, Esmelia stopped the broom, hovering in the air just above the treetops, looking for a way in. Among jagged rocks, the main doors were wide open, the cavernous entrance hall glowing with lights. "Ha, that's a trap, that is," she muttered to herself. "And a rubbish one and all."

In front of her, Ringo jumped up and down to attract her attention. Esmelia's gaze followed the direction his leg was pointing. High in the tallest turret, looking out onto deadly rocks, so far above the ground that no hair-climbing prince could ever reach it, a window was open. Behind the window, all was in darkness.

Esmelia looked down at the little beetle. "That's her room is it?"

Ringo bobbed.

"Knows you was coming to get me, does she?"

Ringo bobbed again.

"So she's probably left it open hoping I'll show up, eh? Probably got a nice cup of tea waiting, too."

More bobbing.

"Quite a useful little fella really, ain't you? Not like some I could mention." Esmelia scowled over her shoulder at Tiddles, who took no notice and washed his ears. As far as cats are concerned, being useful is way beneath them.

Poking at her skirt with a gnarly finger, Esmelia hissed, "Quiet in there you lot. No croaking. And get ready to start Operation Getting Out of Esmelia's Knickers." Rapping her knuckles on the wooden handle, she said, "Alright, off you goes broom." With the old witch clinging to it, the broomstick shot towards the Bleak Fortress, circled the tower once, swooped through the window and came to an abrupt halt, throwing Esmelia onto the floor in a jumble of old black clothes with Ringo buzzing around her head.

Under Esmelia's skirts, a frog immediately wriggled free, gasped for a breath of fresh air and hopped under the bed.

"Hullo Esmelia," purred a voice.

Esmelia's head shot up. Her jaw dropped as she spotted her apprentice sitting in a leather chair by the glowing embers of the fire. Sam looked like Esmelia had never seen her before. For a start, she was clean. Her hair fell in a dark shining river over her shoulders, her dress shimmered in the dim light and her lips curved in a welcoming smile.

With a jolt, Esmelia realised that there was a strange, and not unpleasant, feeling in her chest. *I ain't pleased to see her,* she told herself sternly. *It's indigestion.*

Sam held up a finger for Ringo to land on, and kissed his tiny face. "Thank you," she whispered for his ears only. "You did well. Now hide. Quickly."

Obediently, the beetle crawled down the front of her dress.

Looking back at Esmelia, she said, louder, "Have you come to rescue me from Diabolica's evil clutches?"

"Pah, I'll show *her* evil clutches," Esmelia replied. "My evil fingers clutching her throat." As the old witch stood, a frog lifted the hem of her dress and wriggled under the wardrobe. Fixing Sam with a beady stare, Esmelia said, "My my my. Ain't *you* looking all la-di-dah."

"Well isn't this *wonderful,*" interrupted a chocolatey voice behind her. "Here we all are, together again."

Her foot narrowly missing another frog that was easing its way out from beneath Esmelia's dress, Diabolica stepped out from the shadows on a waft of expensive perfume and put a hand on Sam's shoulder. "You've put on weight Esmelia," she smiled "Your bottom looks enormous."

14
A Witch and Her Apprentice

Another frog escaped from Esmelia's underwear. Unseen, it hopped away into the shadows, coughing. The old witch ignored it and scowled at Sam through the gloom, her mind buzzing like a wasps nest. *This is one o' them times when a witch has to say something sharp and nasty,* she thought to herself. As she racked her brain for something that would put Diabolica and Sam firmly in their place a frog croaked under her dress.

"How *utterly* revolting," murmured Diabolica.

Realising that the moment for saying sharp and nasty things had passed, Esmelia ignored Diabolica. Glaring at Sam she hissed, "Like that then is it? Lured poor, dear Esmelia into a trap has you? Dirty work, treachery and darkest betrayal, is it?"

"Yup," Sam said with a smile that dripped sweetness. "That just about covers it."

"Going to have me dragged off to the deepest, darkest, dreariest dungeon is you?"

"Again, spot on," smiled Sam.

"Gone evil eh?"

Her apprentice clapped. "Very good," she said. "Three out of three."

"Well, about time you turned nasty," replied Esmelia, straightening up. "I always said you was too much of a dopey, saving-baby-birds, wobbly-lip type of drip to be a proper witch. Only one thing wrong with that, though."

Sam tipped her head to one side. "And what might that be?" she asked.

"Witchin' law number 2,346, section 3 clause b," said Esmelia sharply. "The apprentice *must* obey the witch at all times."

"She's not your apprentice," snapped Diabolica. "She's *my* daughter."

"Oh yeah," sneered Esmelia. "We'll see

about that. *You,*" she barked, pointing a bony finger at Sam, "go and clean out the cat's litter tray."

Sam was on her feet before she knew what she was doing. She blinked, confused.

"Sit," hissed Diabolica, pushing down on Sam's shoulder. "She can't order you to do *anything*. She has no *real* power. No *magic*. She is *nothing.*"

Sam sat, her face grim.

"She's my apprentice," said Esmelia stubbornly, "only me and the Most Superior High and Wicked Witch can break that. It's the law. And seeing as the Most Superior High and Wicked Witch is me as well, she can whistle if she thinks I'm lettin' her wriggle out of it."

"Those are the old laws," yawned Diabolica. "After I am crowned tomorrow night, there will be just one law. *Mine.* No more Most Superior High and Wicked Witch, no more silly trials. Just me, the Wicked but Lovely Witch Queen of All the World, with Samantha at my side. What do you say darling?" she asked stroking Sam's hair. "Would you like to be thrown in a dungeon with scabby old Esmelia or rule the world with mummy?"

"Oh, I'll go with Esmelia I think."

Diabolica gasped.

Hope burned in Esmelia's eyes.

"Just kidding," giggled Sam. "I wanted to see the look on her face. Stupid old bag thought I might actually mean it. Mwah ha ha and all that."

With a snarl, Esmelia folded her arms. "Pah," she spat. "After everything I done for you you ungrateful little maggot."

A frog dropped down her leg and hopped to safety. It didn't particularly care where, so long as it was nowhere near Esmelia's pants.

Esmelia's fingers twitched. With a snap, forty witches would suddenly appear. *That'd knock the snooty look off their faces,* she thought to herself. Something stopped her clicking though. For a start, while forty witches would appear two would be squashed under the bed, one under the wardrobe, and another under the chest of drawers. The rest were still in her knickers. Thirty-six frogs suddenly becoming full-size witches in her underwear with a *pouff* of glittery smoke would *definitely* have the element of surprise. The question was: *who* would be the most surprised, Diabolica and Sam, the knicker witches, or Esmelia herself?

And there was something else. Something that made Esmelia pause in her clicking. Although she always thought of her apprentice as a snivelling goody-goody, she had to admit the little toad could cook up a fiendish plan like a proper witch when it suited her. Sam had betrayed her at the Most Superior High and Wicked Witch trials, and then tricked Diabolica too.

Plus, Sam had started to obey when she had been given an order. The bond between witch and apprentice was still there.

Esmelia's eyes flicked from Sam to Diabolica and back again. She was quite sure that Sam was betraying *someone,* but for the life of her, she couldn't work out who.

"I knew you'd come," Sam said, looking up at Esmelia with one eye twitching ever so very slightly. "I knew you wouldn't be able to stop yourself meddling and busybodying and sticking your big, warty nose in."

Did she just wink at me? "I've told you a million times," Esmelia snapped. *"I'm* a wicked witch. *Wicked witch* dearie. That's what we do. And *you,"* she continued slowly, prodding Sam in the chest, "are about as evil as a custard pie."

"Shut up. I *am* evil," hissed Sam furiously.

"Rubbish. If you was evil you'd have stopped gabblin' and done something like this by now."

The sound of the slap echoed around the room.

Sam gasped and held her hand to her cheek. Her eyes glistened with tears.

As she saw the expression of shock and hurt in Sam's eyes, Esmelia knew for certain *exactly* who Sam was planning to betray. Dropping her hand, she stepped back. Another frog dropped down her leg. "Let's get on with it then," she said, sticking out her chin. "Dungeons and whatnot. Least I won't have to look at you two primping ninnies."

"Guards…" Diabolica shouted.

"No, allow me mother. I've always wanted to do this," Sam interrupted. "Guards! *Guards!*"

Nothing happened.

Sighing, Sam yelled, "Brain-dead shuffling zombie things! Brain-dead shuffling zombie things!"

The door crashed open. Two zombie-witches shuffled in, moaning "Di-a-bol-i-ca."

"Take her," commanded Sam, pointing at Esmelia. She glanced at the bed. "And the little cat too. Throw them into the deepest, darkest, *dreariest,* dungeon."

"I'll get you for this, you see if I don't," Esmelia spat, shaking her fist at Sam as she was pushed out of the door.

"They all say that when they've been betrayed,"

said Diabolica. "I suppose it makes them feel slightly better but it's tremendously difficult to get anyone when you're locked up in a dungeon."

Sam watched as Esmelia was dragged away. Watched as another frog appeared beneath the hem of Esmelia's skirts. Watched as it hurried to hide. She frowned. Then her eyes widened. Diabolica had been right, the old witch's bottom was enormous. She was smuggling frogs. Frogs that would never be noticed among the hundreds already leaping about the Bleak Fortress.

Esmelia had just moved an army into the Bleak Fortress. In her knickers. Right under Diabolica's nose.

Throwing back her head, Sam laughed. Not an evil "mwah ha ha" laugh, but the laugh of a girl who has just heard a good joke.

"Are you quite alright darling?" asked Diabolica.

Sam twirled round and grinned at her mother. "Oh yes," she sparkled. "I like having people thrown in the dungeons. It's fun."

15

In Diabolica's Dressing Room

A cold sun climbed into the sky and peered down on a world of frosted white. Looking like a half-eaten wedding cake that had gone a bit nasty, the Bleak Fortress slept. The creatures of the night were… well… creatures of the night. Come daybreak most had melted into the castle's shadowy places to wait for the dark to return. A few, however, remained wakeful. Never-sleeping zombie-witches shuffled along corridors, struggling under giant rolls of red carpet and candles the size of lamp posts as they prepared for the coronation. Others took down portraits of Most Superior High and Wicked Witches to throw on a bonfire in the courtyard.

In private chambers, the soon-to-be Wicked But Lovely Witch Queen of All the World paced up and down. Sensibly, she was wearing a dress that wasn't too tight and was, therefore, striding across the vast floor of her palatial bedroom at quite a good speed, pausing every now and then to kick a frog out of the way. Like every good pacer up-and-downer, she was deep in thought. It had finally arrived: the Midwinter Moon, the day she had been waiting and planning for since she had found out that she had magical power. When midnight struck, she would be crowned. *So why am I not completely happy?* Diabolica thought to herself. *Why have I got the heebie-jeebies?*

She sat at her dressing table. Picking up a ruby encrusted brush, she ran it through her already perfect hair and gazed into the mirror. Mr Popsy tinkled among crystal bottles of perfume. Diabolica frowned. Everything was not what it seemed.

Something that Esmelia had said before she had been dragged off to the dungeons had woken the worm of doubt at the back of her mind. And although she couldn't quite put her finger on what was troubling her, she hadn't become a power-crazed evil sorceress out to take over the world by ignoring the wriggling worm of doubt at the back of her mind.

Diabolica concentrated hard. *Yes. That's it,* she thought to herself: *"and* you *are about as evil as a custard pie."* That's what the old cauldron-botherer had said.

Leaning forward. Diabolica frowned and passed a hand across the mirror. "Show me my daughter," she whispered.

Her reflection faded away. It was replaced by an image of Sam, in her room. The demon-carved bed was piled with dresses. Sam was holding a gown of shark skin and rare white squirrel fur to herself and twirling to judge its swish factor. Diabolica smiled faintly. It was something she did herself. She, too, liked frocks that had plenty of swish.

Her daughter was simply choosing a dress for the coronation. There was nothing there to worry about.

As Diabolica watched, Sam stopped swishing and tapped her wand against her cheek. *Just like her mother,* smiled Diabolica again. *I'm just being foolish,* she told herself firmly. *What does Esmelia Sniff know about anything?* "Look at me, twitching like a twittery pigeon Mr Popsy," she giggled softly. "Just because in a few hours time I'm going to become the first Wicked but Lovely Witch Queen of All the World for a thousand years. Aren't I a big silly?"

The kitten purred at the sound of its mistress's voice, and knocked a bottle of perfume over. Diabolica righted it and picked her familiar up, rubbing her nose against Mr Popsy's soft coat. "I should do something to calm down," she told the kitten. "Maybe I should go and break Esmelia's legs. That would be relaxing, wouldn't it?"

As Diabolica stretched out her hand to change the mirror back. Something made her stop. She frowned.

Behind Sam stood Helza.

Igor.

Diabolica stroked the kitten and tried to puzzle out what was making her stare at her ex-apprentice. Helza was shuffling about Sam's room with her mouth hanging open, hands hanging like claws at her side, exactly as zombies were supposed to. Except... except... there was something about her that wasn't *quite* like the other zombie-witches.

Looks neat, doesn't she, whispered the worm.

While the other zombie-witches were all caked with filth, Helza's face was clean. Sam had washed her. Sam had *cared* for her.

Diabolica leaned back, Esmelia's words coming back to her again: *"and you are about as evil as a custard pie."*

The Black Wand of Ohh Please Don't Turn Me

Into Aaaarghh… Ribbett tapped against Diabolica's cheek as she stared at Sam in her mirror. "Is it possible, Mr Popsy, that she's not evil after all?" she said quietly.

Mr Popsy chased his own tail, knocking over more twinkling bottles on Diabolica's dressing table. This time, she ignored them. "Oh, don't be so ridiculous, Diabolica," she said to herself eventually. "Samantha *must* be evil. She turned her best friend into a zombie, and did the proper 'mwah ha ha HA!' laugh while she did it."

Yes, but was that really evil? said the worm.

In the mirror, Sam tossed the fabulously expensive dress into a corner while Helza passed her another. Diabolica rested her chin in the palm of her hand and stared. Helza *was* a zombie, that much was true. But it was also true that she had escaped the torturing that Diabolica had planned for her. Apart from the whole shuffly drooly thing, she hadn't been harmed at all. In fact, she had been released from her dungeon and, since then, Sam had kept Helza close at all times. Almost as if she were keeping an eye on her friend. Almost as if she were *protecting* her.

And she took Igor's anti-zombification potion, said the worm.

Diabolica raised one delicate eyebrow as she realised that Sam could break the spell over her friend at any time she chose.

Seconds ticked by.

"No, I'm wrong. It doesn't mean anything," said Diabolica, getting up and pacing again. "She betrayed Esmelia and had her thrown into the dungeon. And… and…"

Try as she might, Diabolica couldn't think of any other way in which Sam had proved her wickedness. There had been plenty of evil glints in her eyes, lots of mwah ha ha-ing and a fair bit of gloating. Even some rubbing the hands together in sinister glee. But, now Diabolica came to think about it, very little *actual* wickedness. Even having Esmelia thrown into the dungeon wasn't exactly evil, Diabolica realised. *She* would have turned the old bag into an earwig and stamped on her, but strangely that had never come up. Sam had taken charge. It had been Sam who had commanded the zombie things to take her down to the deepest, darkest, dreariest dungeon, and the deepest, darkest, dreariest dungeon wasn't much worse than Esmelia's cottage. And with Esmelia in the deepest, darkest, dreariest dungeon Sam would know exactly where she was if, for instance, she wanted to hatch a plot with her.

"No," snapped Diabolica. She stopped pacing. "Samantha *is* evil. The truth potion. She told me she was evil. She *must* be evil ..."

And what could be more evil than betraying your own mother?

Diabolica spun around. Grasping the edge of the dressing table with both hands she stared into the mirror. The room was now empty. Sam and Helza had vanished. "Show me my daughter," Diabolica screamed, waving her hand quickly across the mirror.

The image changed. Now it showed nothing but inky blackness.

"Curses," Diabolica cried, sweeping her arm across the surface of the dressing table. In a crash of shattering glass and a mewing of a frightened kitten, she stood tall, eyes blazing. "How?" she demanded. "How did she lie through a truth potion? It's *impossible.*"

16
Dark Passages

Sam lifted a hand. The darkness was so completely dark that she couldn't see it in front of her face. Keeping her other hand on the damp stone of the wall beside her, she took a careful step forward. Something scurried away. Cobwebs snapped across her face. "Gross," she whispered. She took another step, this time feeling a stone step beneath her foot. Just as Gruselda the Skanky's plan of the Bleak Fortress had said, the secret passage led downwards, into a network of other passages, one of which led straight to the deepest, darkest, dreariest dungeon. "Helza," she whispered. "Put your hand on my shoulder. I'll lead you down."

"Saaaaam," said a voice in the darkness. The shuffling sound of Helza's dragging footsteps stopped suddenly. "Saaa…"

Helza began to tumble down the steps. Lunging forwards, Sam caught the zombie-witch around the waist in the darkness and pulled her upright. "Sheesh," she said. "This is going to be tricky."

Groping for Helza's hand in the darkness, she held it tight and led her down another step. Once again, Helza shuffled and stumbled. Once again, Sam clutched at her in the darkness. "Drat, this is going to take forever. I thought you zombies were good at shuffling about in the dark," Sam muttered. "Oh well, it's nearly time anyway." With a rustling sound she dipped a hand down the front of her dress. There was a tiny pop as she pulled the cork. "Drink this," she said. Putting the bottle to her friend's mouth she poured.

"Waaaaa…jeeepersflipppincreepers," Helza shouted. "It burns, it burns!"

"Shhhhh, be *quiet*. Someone, some*thing,* might hear you," hissed Sam.

"Saaaa… Sorry, *Sam?*"

"Yes. It's OK, you're alright. It's just the anti-zombification potion making you feel like your head's going to burst."

"You turned me into a *zombie,*" said Helza. In the dark, her voice shook with fury. "How *could* you?"

"Wait, before you…"

"Let me tell you," Helza interrupted with outraged fury. "There are some things that friends just do *not* do, and top of that list is turning each other into the brainless, undead, grovelling spawn of evil."

"Please be quiet Helza. I know you're upset about the whole zombie thing but… "

"Uh-uh, I will *not* be quiet. I thought we were, like, friends and that. Clearly, I was humungo-wrongo."

"I'm sorry. OK? Believe me, if there was any other way to keep you safe, I would have done it," whispered Sam urgently. She found her friend's hand in the darkness and gave it a squeeze. "Now, please please please be quiet."

"Safe!" yelled Helza, snatching her hand away. "You call that *safe?* It was horrible. It was like being a geography teacher. I knew what I was doing, and I knew it was wrong, but I couldn't stop. *Horrible. And* you made me bang my head against the wall."

"It was better than Diabolica torturing you, and I had to make it look like I really was nasty."

"Well, let me tell you, you really *are* nasty," Helza snarled.

Sam sighed. "We are at *war,*" she said quietly. "By turning you into a zombie I saved you from the torture chamber *and* made Diabolica trust me. If I had to, I'd do exactly the same again. There was *no* other way. Understand?"

"Oh," said Helza, startled. "You're, like, a double agent style of thing?"

"Yes," whispered Sam with another sigh. "I have been pretending to be wicked in order to defeat my own long-lost mother and end her reign of terror, which hasn't – you know – really begun yet, but it'll be pretty terrifying if it does."

"You're not raving bonkers evil then?"

"No," said Sam quietly. Remembering how good it had felt to use the black magic, she added, "Not *very* evil anyway. Now, would you *please* whisper."

"So, if you were, uh, just trying to fool Diabolica, why didn't you unzombie me earlier?" Helza asked, finally lowering her voice. "I could have *acted* zombie. I'm *awesome* at acting."

"Too dangerous. All it would have taken was one small slip and Diabolica would have guessed."

For a moment, neither spoke while Helza thought about what Sam had told her. She could see the sense of it, and deep down, Helza was a sensible young woman despite having purple hair. She had also been Diabolica's apprentice for a long time and had survived those years by pretending to be a loyal servant. "Hmmm, OK," she said eventually. "Well maybe I can find it in my heart to, like, forgive you. *Maybe.*"

"Gee thanks," Sam muttered.

"One more question," whispered Helza, holding

up a finger, which was, of course, completely pointless, the passage being, as it was, completely dark. "Why are we standing around in the dark? It's *really* creepy."

"Secret passage," whispered Sam. "I've got to see Esmelia…"

"And you've forgotten how to do a light spell? Here, let me."

"No," said Sam quickly, reaching out and clutching at Helza's arm. "Diabolica has eyes everywhere. Especially now. Ghouls and wraiths and things. We've got to be fast and we *cannot* be seen."

"OK," whispered Helza, "but if I get spiders in my hair I am going to scream."

In the darkness, Sam smiled. "One more thing," she whispered. "The coronation is tonight. When we get out of here I want you to keep out of sight. It's too risky to let Diabolica see you now and I have a plan."

"A plan?"

"Yes," said Sam. "I thought that I could *steal* The White Wand of… Oi You Could Have Someone's Eye Out With That but then I had a better idea. Diabolica is going to *give* it to me."

"And then what?"

"And then," whispered Sam. "The war *really* starts."

"Cool. What can I do?"

"Well, some more of this excellent potion might come in handy," said Sam shaking the almost empty bottle.

"Ingredients?"

"Leave it to me. Now, put your hand on my shoulder, be careful where you put your feet and be *quiet.*"

One step at a time, Sam lead Helza down. As she turned along twisting passages things crawled in the darkness. Helza gritted her teeth as spiders dropped into her hair. But the passageway was secret, safe. Ever downwards they went until, at last, they heard singing in the distance. A song that Sam had heard many times before back in Pigsnout Wood. It was a soft, sad little number...

> *I can't get my finger out of your head*
> *It's stuck right inside your eye sock-ettt*
> *No, I can't get my finger out of your head*
> *I'll have to put my foot on your neck and wiggle*
> *it around a bit...*

"Esmelia!" hissed Sam through the bars of the door.

"Eh? Eh? What?" Esmelia had lit a small fire from straw and – Sam was horrified to see – skeleton bones. In the light of the flames she looked up and moaned, "Oh, I wondered when you'd get here."

17

The Storm Before the Storm

Surrounded by glass bottles and jars twenty times as big as himself, Ringo heaved. A bottle of black powder shifted slightly. Wiping a leg across his brow, he braced his back against the side of the wooden cabinet and heaved again. This time, the bottle rocked forward, and slowly toppled. The little beetle watched as it spun end over end and shattered on the stone floor among the broken glass of several others.

Ringo held his breath, listening. All was silent. No-one came running in shouting "Help! Help! There's a beetle robbing the potions store!" No-one in the Bleak Fortress was worried about a few old bottles of drying herbs and dragon spit and dried brain and gunpowder. Fluttering to the floor, Ringo pushed a small heap of the powder into the centre of a black handkerchief. Carefully folding it, he gripped it between his pincers and spread his wings.

The passageways of the Bleak Fortress were filling up. As the sun set, black hooded figures poured into the corridors, their voices whispering like wind through gravestones. "It hasss come. Now iss the time for sssssuffering," they rasped. And, "Hurry up, we wantsss to get good sssseatsss."

On the floor, flopping along between the feet of the undead, frogs, too, made their way towards the Great Throne Room.

Along the length of the corridor, candles blazed, creating pools of light. Just like any other insect in a castle that was alive with creepy-crawlies, Ringo buzzed from shadow to shadow, past heavy-footed demons and new portraits of Diabolica.

A werewolf snapped. Fangs set in a snarling muzzle closed inches away from Ringo. With a surge of effort, the little beetle zipped away and rested for a moment on the sculpture of Pandora Box. It had been too heavy for the zombie-witches to move so, instead, they had put a bag over Pandora's head. Panting, Ringo put down the hankie of black powder and made a mental note to add a few sentences to *Ringo: Beetle of Destiny*. By the time he had picked up the handkerchief again, he had decided it would be a full chapter featuring a desperate beetle versus werewolf fight to the death.

THE WILD WINTER

Beyond the tall, arched window of Sam's room a full moon was rising. A small cauldron bubbled on the fire. Helza stirred it slowly. Sam peered through a crack in the door. Glancing over her shoulder nervously, she whispered, "How much longer?"

"Hey, it's not like making a banana smoothie. It takes time, and I *need* more gunpowder," Helza hissed back. "Where's that beetle?"

Puffing a little, Ringo took to the air again. A little further down the passage, he could see the staircase that led up into Sam's tower. Zig-zagging through demon horns he flew, buzzing around shaggy heads with three eyes and resting briefly on the brim of a hat worn by a walking skeleton who was trying to cover his bald spot.

Almost there.

Suddenly, the crowd parted. Ringo put on another burst of speed, racing for the spiralling staircase. Straight as an arrow he flew…

…. straight into the face of Diabolica Nightshade.

"Ugh," said Diabolica, doggy-paddling her hands in front of her face. "Disgusting. As if I haven't got enough problems the stupid castle is full of insects."

Slapped away by one of her flailing hands, Ringo smashed against the wall. Dazed, he dropped his precious handkerchief and fell to the floor, on his back. He could do nothing but waggle his legs in the air and spin in circles as Diabolica swished past.

Upside down, the little beetle watched as Diabolica took the stairs to Sam's room.

The door slammed open. Framed in the doorway, Diabolica stared at Sam, her face like a hailstorm.

"Mother!" giggled Sam. "How nice to see you. What do you think?" She spun in the middle of the room swishing the skirts of her dress.

Diabolica leaned against the wall and narrowed her eyes as her gaze swept around the mess. A cheerful fire blazed in the hearth. In the corner Helza was banging her head against the wall. "It smells funny in here," Diabolica said.

"Yes, it's Igor," Sam said wrinkling her nose. "I think she's been eating rats again. Igor," she snapped over her shoulder, "would you stop doing that. It's giving me a headache."

"Hmmm," said Diabolica, watching Helza closely as she slumped in the corner droning "Saaaam."

"Do you like it?" Sam repeated, her lips pursing into a slightly annoyed pout. She twirled again. "Aren't you *proud?*"

Slowly, Diabolica looked her daughter up and down, taking in the dress of darkest moth-wing velvet. Her scowl deepened.

"Mother? Is everything alright?"

The corners of Diabolica's mouth twitched. Suddenly, she knew what Sam had done with the truth potion. Suddenly, everything was clear. Suddenly, she felt much, *much* better. Sam might have tried to outwit her again, just like at the Most Superior High and Wicked Witch Trial, but this time she – Deadly Nightshade – wouldn't be outwitted. This time *she* would be the outwitterer. And she would teach her daughter a thing or two about outwittering. Diabolica's smile grew wider. "Why yes," she replied. "I'm *fine* dear. Everything is absolutely fine."

"I said, aren't you proud of me," said Sam twirling in her dress again.

Diabolica's smile broadened. "Samantha darling," she said softly. "I couldn't have wished for a daughter as beautiful as you."

Sam grinned. Turning back to her mother she said, "Was there something you wanted?"

"Just to remind you not to be late," said Diabolica silkily. "Tonight's the big night, and I have a little surprise for you."

"Oh, I love surprises," said Sam, clapping her hands together. "Are you going to fire Esmelia out of a cannon? Can I chain her to a hungry tiger? Can I have a clue?"

Diabolica held up her finger with a smile as she turned away. "Ah a aah," she giggled over her shoulder. "No clues. It's a *surprise.*"

The hoof of a passing demon sent Ringo spinning against the wall again. This time, he landed on his feet. Scrambling through the shuffling feet of zombie-witches and clicking claws and toes of bone and webbed feet, he found the precious handkerchief of gunpowder and turned for the stairs just in time to see Diabolica step down. Smiling, she nodded to bowing minions as she passed.

Ringo shuddered and spread his wings once more and zoomed up the spiralling stairs.

"She *knew* Helza. I'm telling you, she knew," hissed Sam as Helza struggled to lift the boiling cauldron out of the wardrobe.

Her friend settled the black pot back on the coals, muttering, "Pheww, it hasn't gone all claggy." Glancing up at Sam she said, "She didn't know anything."

"But didn't you see her face? She looked like Mr Popsy had done his business in her handbag."

"Pah," replied Helza. "I used to live with her, remember? She *always* looks like that. Plus, underneath all the hair and jewels she really is as dumb as a brick."

Sam plonked her bottom on the bed. "You're probably right," she said. "I'm scared and I don't want to fight her. She's my mother and a very powerful sorceress."

"Not as powerful as you," said Helza calmly, stirring the pot. "And, sorry I have to say this, but she's a *really* bad mom."

Sam grinned. "What is the difference between a witch and a sorceress anyway?" she asked.

"Hats," said Helza simply, glad to have brought a smile to Sam's face. "Sorceresses don't wear pointy hats." She glancing towards the door. "Ah, here's the beetle. You took your time dude."

"Hats? Is that it?"

"Yup," said Helza. "Now, like, shut up. I totally need to concentrate on this bit."

18
Midwinter Moon

The Great Throne Room was packed. Taking a deep breath, Sam stepped onto the red carpet. Washed in golden light, eerie faces drooled and gibbered as she walked on trembling knees past rows of Diabolica's creatures. Down the sides of the room, magical herbs burned in great dishes, adding heavy perfume to air that was already thick with the stench of the grave and – thanks to the werewolves – the smell of wet dog. At the end of the carpet a new Great Throne had been raised on a stage. This one had been carved from crystal and padded with cushions of silk embroidered with silver thread. Behind it stood ranks of zombie-witches.

She glanced out of the window. In the star-spangled sky, the Midwinter Moon rode higher.

Midnight was close.

Sam walked on. As she passed, creatures bowed and scraped and grovelled. Sam ignored them. Somewhere close by was The White Wand of... Oi You Could Have Someone's Eye Out With That. She could feel it. Her heart pounded and her blood fizzed with magical longing. Forcing herself to stay calm, she swished down the red carpet and stood before her own small throne, wondering for a moment why she, too, hadn't been given a new one. Pushing the thought to one side, she gazed over the sea of furred, scaled, horned and hooded creatures. Even the vast throne room couldn't hold them all. Through the window, more were crowded into the courtyard, dragons perched on the Bleak Fortress's turrets.

Her heart sank. Soon, she would have to fight them all. Alone.

No, not quite alone, Sam thought, glancing down at the beetle on her shoulder. With a small smile, she lifted her eyes and watched as frogs hopped through the shadows.

In a distant corner of the Bleak Fortress, a zombie-witch droned, "Di-a-bol-i-ca," as she shuffled towards the throne room. A hand reached out and dragged her into a dark passageway.

"Di-a-bol-ooomph."

There was a pause. Then, in the darkness: "Wark! Me toes is curling…"

"Shhhh, no time for that," whispered Helza. "Take this," she said pressing a small glass bottle into the witch's hand. "And listen very carefully."

The massive doors of the Great Throne Room groaned open. Dressed in a gown of purest white satin with a high collar, Diabolica entered the room. A hush swept across the guests. For a moment there was silence and then the ranks of zombie-witches behind Sam burst into song. "Di-a-bol-i-ca" they chanted in a horrible clash of notes and tunes, "Di-a-bol-i-*caaaaa.*"

Diabolica picked her way along the red carpet. Behind her came a procession of ghouls and zombies and beasts. A demon carried a cushion of white velvet in his claws. On the cushion rested a tall, spiky crown of white gold and diamonds.

Behind the demon, drifted a wraith carrying a second cushion, this one of deepest black. Sam's fingers clenched around sweaty palms. On the black cushion, glittering gently, was The White Wand of... Oi You Could Have Someone's Eye Out With That. Tearing her eyes away from it with an effort, Sam dropped a curtsey as Diabolica walked up the steps to her new throne. For a mad moment, she fought down an urge to confess her plans and beg her mother's forgiveness. Darkness swirled about her, whispering to her. She clenched her teeth together, trying to ignore it, and forced a bright smile onto her face.

Diabolica nodded to her once, turned to the hall and raised her hands for silence.

The zombie-witch chanting stopped. The Great Throne Room fell silent once more. Diabolica swept The Black Wand of Ohh Please Don't Turn Me Into Aaaarghh... Ribbett in a glittering trail of black and purple. When she spoke her voice was magically loud. Loud enough to be heard in the courtyard below. Loud enough to shake the windows.

"Tonight is the night of the Midwinter Moon," said Diabolica, her whisper roaring through the hall, "The night of blackest magic. Tonight, begins a new age of darkness. Tonight, all my years of plots and schemes and poisoning off Old Biddy Vicious and befrogginating Cakula von Drakula finally bear fruit. Zombie-witches and wraiths and ghouls and demons and dragons will soon be released, to spread havoc. Thousands of nightmare creatures will bring a world that no longer believes in darkness to its knees. Magic will blaze again. Tonight, I become the world's new Queen. Tonight, we drench the world in *evil!*"

As one, the creatures of the night rose to their feet, clapping paws and hooves and claws. The Great Throne Room shook with howls of approval.

Diabolica spread her arms for quiet.

"Tonight," she continued. "We will show them all that magic is *real*. Tonight the Earth is *ours,* though – obviously – when I say 'ours' I mean *mine* really."

Windows cracked as the roaring of the guests reached new peaks.

In the distance, the Bleak Fortress's clock began its gloomy chime. Midnight had arrived. "But first the crown," said Diabolica, silencing the room again. "And as there is no-one in this world worthy to place it upon my head, I shall just have to do it myself."

The crowd parted. The demon came forward and

kneeled before Diabolica. Holding up the cushion, he said, "I, Lord Freakish Throatwringer, Duke of the Slimy Pit, do have the honour of presenting to thee the crown of the Wicked but Lovely Witch Queen of…"

"Shut up," hissed Diabolica, snatching the crown from its cushion. "It's not all about *you.*"

Cringing, Lord Throatwringer scuttled backwards.

Diabolica held the dazzlingly bejewelled crown high. "Behold," she cried in the voice of storms. "The crown of the Wicked but Lovely Witch Queen of All the World."

As the creatures howled once more, the zombie-witches lifted silver trumpets to their lips and blew a fanfare that, frankly, sounded like a group of musicians warming up, badly. Diabolica glared over her shoulder at them until they stopped. And then she lowered the crown until it rested atop her shining mane of hair.

"Bow to me," she cried. "Grovel before your *queen.*"

As every creature in the hall hurried to obey her, Diabolica waved The Black Wand of Ohh Please Don't Turn Me Into Aaaarghh… Ribbett until the black and purple glitter filled the air. And then, she tipped back her head and laughed.

"Mwah ha ha HA HA HA HA!"

Sam clutched her ears as every window in the Bleak Fortress shattered.

The sound echoed over valleys of Transylvania and swept through the meadows and plains. Across land and seas Diabolica's laugh thundered, flooding the world. With it went streaks of wild black magic, blazing and dancing and boiling and glittering darkly through the skies. In every corner of the globe, people dropped mugs of tea on the floor or awoke chewing their duvet in horror, or ran to hide under the dog's basket. And still the enormous laugh of the world's new queen filled the sky: a warning, and a promise of doom soon to arrive.

Diabolica lowered her chin. Eyes shining with wicked glee, she settled herself upon the Crystal Throne. As the last echoes of her laugh died away, she turned her head and looked at Sam. "And now," she said. "I have a surprise for my daughter." She crooked a finger and the wraith carrying the black cushion came forward. Like the demon, he kneeled, whispering "Your *majesssty,*" in a voice like sandpaper.

Sam's eyes opened wide as Diabolica bent forward and lifted The White Wand of… Oi You Could Have Someone's Eye Out With That. She took a gulp of air to stop herself panting. The time had come to fight.

No, the darkness screamed. *Join with Diabolica, rule alongside your mother. You are powerful...*

"You once told me that when you made this wand it became white because you are *good*," said Diabolica, interrupting her thoughts.

Sam looked up, surprised, into her mother's eyes. Did Diabolica know that she had been deceived? Had she guessed? Heart beating furiously, Sam choked, "No, no. *Evil* now."

Diabolica held the wand out, it's tip pointing directly at Sam's heart. "Yes, evil," said Diabolica as her daughter's trembling hand reached out to take it.

Sam's fingers were an inch away when Diabolica muttered under her breath. A blast of magic smashed into Sam's chest, knocking her off the stage, sending her sprawling onto her backside on the cold stone. "Evil enough to betray your own *mother*," Diabolica hissed, glaring at Sam poisonously.

"But – but ..."

"Silence!" Diabolica threw the wand into the air where it spun for a moment, throwing off sparkles like a Catherine wheel before she caught it again. Blowing on the tip, she looked at the front row of her creatures and slaves. "Well," she yelled. "What are you waiting for.

Sieze her."

Sam struggled as claws and skeleton hands clutched at her, pinning her arms behind her back. Pale as Diabolica's dress, she lifted her face to look into her mother's eyes.

"Surprise," said Diabolica.

19
Witch Queen of All the World

Sam stopped struggling. Undead creatures surrounded her, closing in ever closer in a wave of stinky horridness. Ghouls sank skeleton fingers into her arms, whispering, "pretty girl, we *wantsss* to eat it" through lipless mouths. A werewolf held her tightly from behind with hairy arms like steel traps, its fanged muzzle against her neck. Other creatures crowded in, snuffling and licking beastly lips. The wolfman growled in her ear. Trying to ignore the dog breath and the pain in her chest where the spell had hit, Sam looked up at her mother. "But m-mother," she said in a small voice. "W-Why would you think I'd betray you?"

Diabolica folded her arms. In each of her hands a wand of power, one white, the other black, dropped glitter onto a floor that was littered with broken glass. A freezing breeze stirred her hair. Frogs crept closer. She tutted and said, "Oh purr*lease* Samantha. It took me a while to work out, I must admit, but as I told you, mummy's not *completely* stupid. Oh, and by the way, I think we can drop the whole 'mother' thing now, what with you being a treacherous little worm. 'Your majesty' will do. Or 'your wicked but lovely queeniness' if you prefer."

Lines creased Sam's forehead. She tried her best to look confused, hoping against hope that she might still fool her mother. "B-But the truth potion. *No-one* can lie through a truth potion," she whispered.

Diabolica raised one eyebrow.

"Yes, but you *didn't* lie did you, you cheeky little toad?" Diabolica said. "Everything you told me was the truth. You knew that betraying your very own mother would be a very naughty thing to do so, quite truthfully, you were able to say that you had decided to be bad. Then, when I asked you if you were going to betray me, you said that you 'wouldn't *want* to do that.' Well, hah, perhaps you didn't *want* to but you were still planning to anyway."

She tipped her head to one side and looked at Sam questioningly. "Have I got that about right darling?"

"But I told you I *loved* you, your... ummm... wicked but lovely queeniness."

"No. No, you didn't," Diabolica chuckled. "What you *did* say is that you've always wanted a mother and that I was beautiful. And that was very very clever indeed. You knew how much I love pretty things, and you knew I'd think that saying I was beautiful was the same as saying you loved me. Especially when you were looking up at me with tears shining in those pretty eyes that look so much like mine. But it's *not* the same, *is* it Samantha?" She took a step towards her daughter, sudden fury blazing in her eyes. "Not the same at *all.*"

Sam dropped her head. It was too late. There was no use pretending any more.

"It was the same with all the other questions," Diabolica continued angrily. "You didn't lie, you just twisted the truth into something you knew I'd want to hear." The Wicked but Lovely Witch Queen of All the World paused for a moment. "I suppose I *should* be proud. It was quite a nasty plot. But, *really* Samantha, after everything I've done for you."

Sam lifted her head. "Everything you've done for me?" she sneered. "What would *that* be? Leaving me on the steps of an orphanage? Tossing my grandmother's book on the fire? Burning my home down? Stealing my wand?"

"'Stealing my wand' *your majesty,*" Diabolica prompted, twiddling The White Wand of... Oi You Could Have Someone's Eye Out With That around her fingers. Around her, unnoticed, frogs formed a circle.

"Oh shut up. Just shut up!" shouted Sam, struggling again, more in anger than in the hope of breaking free. "If you're a 'majesty' I'm a jam doughnut."

"You very easily *could* be a jam doughnut," said Diabolica dangerously, tapping The Black Wand of Ohh Please Don't Turn Me Into Aaaarghh… Ribbett against her cheek.

"Hah, go on then," snapped Sam. "Turn me into whatever you like, the same as you do to *everyone* who gets in your way. It won't stop it being the truth. You're not a *queen.* You're not even a decent mother."

Diabolica's face paled. She leaned forward. With icy fury, she purred, "Enough of this silly chit-chat. Take her away."

The creatures closed in, pushing Sam across the stone floor. Struggling was no good. Closing her eyes, Sam summoned magic. When she opened them again, her eyes were dark, black power flooding through her veins. Her lips moved, shaping the words of a spell that would reduce the creatures around her to dust.

"Naughty naughty, we'll have none of that," giggled Diabolica, waving The Black Wand of Ohh Please Don't Turn Me Into Aaaarghh… Ribbett.

Sam's magic vanished. She tried jerking away, but

she was held tight. She kicked and punched but the creatures just laughed, grunting and hissing as they dragged her across the stone floor. "NOW," she yelled.

At the back of the Great Throne Room the doors slammed open. A chill wind rushed through the Great Throne Room, bringing with it an equally chilly cackle: "Nyyyaaaaargh he heh huuuurgghh."

Every head swung round. Diabolica looked up to see a cloaked and bent and raggedy black figure standing beneath the arch of the great doors, outlined in a glow of candlelight, a cat twining around its ankles. The figure was wearing a bent pointed hat and rubbing its hands together.

"Get your filthy beasts off *my* apprentice," roared Esmelia!

"Surprise, mother," yelled Sam.

Diabolica rolled her eyes. "Oh for crying out loud darling, it's only Esmelia Sniff," she purred. "What sort of surprise weapon is Esmelia Sniff? Besides, I've been expecting her."

"Oh yeah?" replied Esmelia. "I bet you weren't expecting *this* though."

She clicked her fingers.

20

Very Dangerous Old Women

Most people, when they look at very old ladies tend to say to themselves, "Oh, look at that poor, feeble, whiskery, old dear. I bet she's a bit forgetful and smells of cabbage and likes china cats." Most people think that old women are a bit useless, just because they're deaf and have rickety legs and faces like unmade beds. What people forget is that very old ladies have had very long lives. They know everything that's worth knowing and they've lived through things that young people can't imagine. They're clever, and they're tough and they can be quite horribly *spiteful.*

In short, old women are dangerous. A good bit of advice, is *never* upset an old lady. And that goes double if the old lady is a witch…

In a circle around Diabolica, forty frogs *pouffed* into glittery smoke that blew away to reveal forty elderly witches, their faces like angry sultanas. None of the witches had liked Diabolica very much to start with, mostly because it was widely felt that she had too many

teeth. Turning a thousand of their fellow witches into zombies had not made her any more popular.

All of them were upset and were spoiling for a fight.

"There she is. Scrag her!" shouted Enid.

"Right you are Enid," replied Dot.

Forty wands pointed at Diabolica. Forty spells screamed through the air trailing sparks.

The new queen stumbled backwards, crown askew, eyes wide and shout of "What the…!" on her perfect lips. She raised both wands. Too slow. A blaze of magic bloomed around her: the magic of forty old, crabby and spiteful witches who – unlike Sam – were all very happy to use whatever magic happened to be swirling about. Light or dark, good or bad, it was all the same to them, so long as it could make Diabolica dance. The battle was not a fight of good against evil. None of Esmelia's army were sparkly, fairy godmothery types. It was a battle of toothless, horrible, damp, smelly, ugly and not-very-nice-at-all against evil.

At the centre of the ring, Wicked but Lovely Witch Queen of All the World screamed, bound by burning ropes of blackest magic. Around the Great Throne Room, creatures of the night cowered and scrambled to the edges of the hall, trying to escape the awful spells.

"Ooo, she don't like that, do she?" screeched one gummy old bag happily.

"Serves her right too," shouted another with a grin.

By the doors of The Great Throne Room, Esmelia rubbed her hands together a bit more and cackled. "That plot was a doozy," she congratulated herself softly. "One of me best. Shame I forgot to bring the scorpion hat." With Diabolica trapped in a web of magic, all she had to do was wander over, pluck The Black Wand of Ohh Please Don't Turn Me Into Aaaarghh… Ribbett from her fingers, taking the other wand too, just to be on the safe side, and hey-presto it was Most Superior High and Wicked Witch time.

Taking a step forward, she shouted, "Aaaaand, *present fingers.*"

Each of the old witches raised a finger into the air. One took a step forward.

"Wait for it, Private Defective. Wait for it," cackled Esmelia, walking towards the Crystal Throne.

A scream from the side of the room. Esmelia's head snapped round. A werewolf was looming over her apprentice, fangs dripping. Without thinking, the old witch changed direction. "Keep Danglybumica busy," she screeched over her shoulder at her army of witches.

"I won't be a moment."

A ghoul stepped in front of her. It pulled back its tattered hood, revealing a hideous face crawling with maggots. "Be afffraid, witch," it hissed.

Esmelia scowled. The ghoul was standing between her and her apprentice. "I never thought I'd say this," she sniffed. "But *you* could do with a *bath* dearie."

A boot lashed out.

"Ouche*sssss,*" hissed the ghoul, stumbling back. "That really hurt*sss.* I hate*ssss* witche*sss.*"

Within seconds Esmelia was surrounded by a scrum of monsters. With fists, boots, knees and fingers she whacked at wraiths, dented demons and gouged ghouls. A skeleton's squealing head bounced away over the stone floor. A werewolf staggered backwards with Tiddles attached to its face.

But for every undead creature Esmelia punched, ten more took their place. And, as she battled, more dread creatures flooded past her.

At the centre of the circle of witches, Diabolica squealed, "Help me. Heeeelp me you cowards. Get the old bags." The words turned into a new scream as fresh magic tore through the air.

"I *knew* I was going to enjoy this war, Enid my

lovely," cackled Dot. "This is even better than punching clowns… Owww, you dirty brute!" She fell in a whirl of teeth and claws as a werewolf pounced.

"Hang on Dot!" cried Enid, dropping her wand. "I'm coming." From beneath her skirts she pulled a frying pan. Wobbling forward on old lady legs, she took a swipe at the wolf's snarling head, yelling, "Naughty doggy. Get in yer basket!"

The magic around Diabolica flickered slightly. "That's it," she screeched. *"Get* them. For your *queen."*

"No," screeched Esmelia. "Don't stop. I ain't got The Black Wand of Ohh Please Don't Turn Me Into Aaaarghh… Ribbett yet. Lunge and poke. *Lunge and poke."* She swung a fist at a demon, and threw herself at the werewolf above Sam. "Down!" she yelled, clutching the beast's heavily furred neck as it tried to sink its teeth into her apprentice. "Down boy! Bad boy!"

The magical bonds that held Diabolica fizzled as she struggled against them. The circle of witches around her was being swamped. One by one, the old women were forced to turn away from the Wicked but Lovely Witch Queen of All the World to defend themselves against the crush of nightmare fiends. The ropes of magic grew dimmer, Diabolica was no longer screaming.

"Yes, my darlings," she shouted. "Fight for your queen. Tear the old ratbags limb from limb."

Slowly but surely, the witches were losing. Soon, only three remained to cast spells at Diabolica. The rest were lost in a heaving mass of fur and tattered black cloaks and scales and teeth and horns, fighting for their lives. The air was filled with unearthly wails and a cry of, "That's right Dot, grab it by the nobbly bits." Toe bones whizzed through the air as a witch beat a hopping skeleton around the head with its own leg.

Soon, only two witches were left to keep Diabolica trapped. Then one.

Zombie witches shuffled forwards to join the fight, with a not-very-impressive battlecry of "Di-a-bol-i-ca." More spells began zipping through the air with *vippp,* and *spang* and *pachooie* noises. The room filled with multi-coloured smoke.

"Free!" screamed Diabolica in triumph as the last of the magic that held her twinkled away to nothing. "Now, Esmelia Sniff you repulsive hag, taste Diabolica's revenge. Prepare to *suffer!*" With a laugh of pure madness, she lifted both wands. The air bubbled with evil.

Pausing only to break a demon's nose, Esmelia twisted her head round in time to see the wands pointing directly at her. "Drat!" she said.

And then the corner of her mouth twitched.

"Finally, I'm going to be free of you, you scabby old trout," Diabolica laughed. "And then the rest of these ridiculous old eyesores. Prepare to meet your doom!"

"Right you are dearie," Esmelia called back with a wink. "Doom and that. Off you goes then."

Diabolica's lips snarled as she formed the word of a spell that would hurl a thousand knives at the old witch. "Stabra… ooof."

The small, blurred shape of a young girl whirred out of the crowd of fighting witches and creatures. A shoulder hit Diabolica in the stomach, fingers clutched at The White Wand of… Oi You Could Have Someone's Eye Out With That.

Panting, Diabolica looked up to see her daughter standing over her.

"Mine I think," Sam said quietly, tapping her wand against her cheek. "Now, two things. First your crown's a bit wonky. Second, are you going to stop this silliness now or do we have to do this the hard way?" Pointing The White Wand of… Oi You Could Have Someone's Eye Out With That at her mother she shrugged and finished calmly, "Well?"

21
Zombies & Dragons & Demons, Oh My!

The fighting stopped. Witches with their hands around ghoul's necks paused in their throttling. Frying pans halted in mid-swing. Roars went unroared and screams unscreamed. Every head in the Great Throne Room turned. All eyes, even the ones that were crawling with maggots, fixed on Diabolica and Sam. Esmelia tried a grin, but quickly remembered that she hadn't managed to grab The Black Wand of Ohh Please Don't Turn Me Into Aaaarghh… Ribbett. She scowled instead and edged forward, telling herself that the battle wasn't over yet and if there was one thing she was good at, apart from breaking fingers, it was stealing. There was still time.

Sam flicked the wand absent-mindedly. A Scab Demon that had been creeping up on her burst into a small flock of white doves. "I *have* learned one or two things from Esmelia you see," Sam said sweetly. "Most importantly, if you're going to hatch a plot, make sure you've got a nasty surprise or two up your sleeve. Was it nasty enough Esmelia?"

"Hurrrumph," hurrumphed Esmelia. "I'd have gone for a finger in the eye. That's classic nasty surprise that is."

Sam ignored her. "And here's another nasty surprise," she said raising her hand.

Secret doors swung open around the Great Throne Room. Spitting cobwebs, ex-zombie-witches poured from passages that hadn't been used for hundreds of years.

Diabolica glanced around the room, her face pale.

"I found the original plans for the Bleak Fortress," her daughter explained. "There's more secret passages than rooms in this place."

Fanning out around the hall, the new troops pointed their wands, standing ready to fight. "Alright bud," Helza shouted happily. "We caught about a hundred. Give us ten minutes and we'll de-zombie the rest." Witches were already waddling forward to pour Helza's potion into the slack mouths of Diabolica's zombies. Within seconds there were shrieks of "Woah Jimmy mind the spanner," and "Wark, wark, wark. Penguin alert" and "Diabolica Nightshade you are going to get a right ding round the ear." One tearful voice sobbed, "Can we go home now, please? We only came to see Randy Stardust and the

Swinging Wowsers."

Sam ignored the commotion, and leaned towards her mother with a smile. "So, your wicked but lovely queeniness, are you going to surrender?" she asked. Quietly, so that only Diabolica could hear her, she added. "I'll make sure you're not treated badly. You're still my mother."

Diabolica's gaze swept across the Great Throne Room again until it rested again on Sam. She lifted her chin. Her nose wrinkled prettily. "You don't seem to have noticed," she said. "But there are two thousand fearsome creatures of the dread netherworld at my command. *Your* army, on the other hand, includes about a hundred and forty rickety-legged old dears, Esmelia Sniff and a silly little girl with a twinkly stick."

Sam frowned.

"I must admit you *did* surprise me Samantha but, frankly, you don't stand a chance." Quicker than the eye could see, she swung The Black Wand of Ohh Please Don't Turn Me Into Aaaarghh… Ribbett. A jet of magic poured from the tip, and curled around Sam.

"Fight!" Diabolica screamed over her shoulder. *"Fight them you fools."*

The brief pause in the battle came to an end.

Fingers tightened around throats. Frying pans went *cloinggggg*. Roars and screams shook the walls of the Bleak Fortress.

Caught within a net of magic, Sam felt her feet becoming longer, her toes spreading. She was getting smaller, her skin turning green and slimy. Her throat was swelling. *"No…*bbit," she croaked, slashing at the air with her own wand. At once, streams of magic around her blasted outwards in every direction. The Crystal Throne toppled and whirled away to smash against the wall. Stone pillars that had stood for a thousand years crashed to the ground. The ceiling groaned and sagged. Ghouls, demons, and an elderly witch were instantly befrogginated wherever Diabolica's magic touched.

"Nice try," said Sam, levelling The White Wand of… Oi You Could Have Someone's Eye Out With That at Diabolica. The carved bone settled into her hand. Sam's shoulders relaxed. She smiled dreamily. With this wand nothing could beat her. She flicked it at her mother.

Diabolica staggered backwards as ribbons of shining white wrapped around her. Snarling, she countered Sam's spell. Another magical explosion shook the Bleak Fortress. Carved stonework crashed from the ceiling, smashing among the fighting armies.

Mother and daughter faced each other: Sam smiling, Diabolica snarling. At the same moment they both waved their wands. Power met in the air between them; a fierce blaze of light and darkness.

The magic of the two most powerful wands the universe had ever seen smashed together. The blast scattered witches and nightmare creatures and blew the ancient doors to the Great Throne Room off their hinges. They whirled away down the corridor as if they were made of paper.

"Dragons," bellowed Diabolica, her hand reaching up like a claw. Her voice shook the castle once more.

Sam was forced to take a step backwards as her mother threw more and more magic into the space between them. She gasped and squeezed her eyes for a moment as the cruelty and evil Diabolica was pouring through The Black Wand of Ohh Please Don't Turn Me Into Aaaarghh… Ribbett threatened to overwhelm her. When she opened them, they were calm again. "Ringo," she said through clenched teeth. "It's time."

The tiny beetle clattered from her shoulder as a dragon landed on a window ledge with a leathery slap of wings that brought more stones tumbling from the ceiling. Roaring, it pushed red and gold scaled shoulders through the ancient stonework. Shrieking witches staggered out of the way as the dragon's head snaked above them. The huge beast opened a mouth lined with teeth like broken gravestones in a roar that made those of the witches who weren't already deaf cover their ears. At the back of the dragon's throat, Sam saw a flicker of fire.

"Make it stop mother," Sam shouted. "It will kill *everyone!*"

"Sorry. Evil. Don't care," Diabolica panted. Smiling grimly she doubled her effort, waving her wand in an complicated and ancient spell.

Sam's concentration was lost. As the force spell glittered around her, she was thrown against a crumbling wall, her head spinning.

Through dazed eyes, Sam looked up. Diabolica stood over her. Her mother's face was twisted with triumph. She saw her raise The Black Wand of Ohh Please Don't Turn Me Into Aaaarghh… Ribbett, magic twinkling at its tip. Behind, the dragon took great a great lungful of air, smoke pouring from its nostrils. When it breathed out, fire would wash over the Great Throne

Room burning everything in its path, both armies would be flamed.

"Dear sweet ladies. *Lovely* ladies. A very good evening to you all."

Diabolica twisted around in shock. Sam blinked. Her dazed eyes focussed. At the end of the room a group of cloaked figures, bristling with heavy wooden staffs, walked through the ruined doors. In front, a heavily bearded man tipped his spangled hat to the witches around him. A smaller, unbearded face peered out nervously from behind his robes.

The man noticed the enormous dragon, his hedgehog eyebrows lifting. "Alright chaps," said Professor Sebastian Dentrifice breezily. "A round of fireballs I think."

"Fireballs *good*," muttered Harry 'Wooden' Legg with satisfaction. "Fireballs go…"

22
Great Balls of Fire

Balls of fire ripped across the Great Throne Room. Younger witches ducked, but the more elderly were slower. The tips of their hats burst into flames. Instead of breathing out fire, a confused dragon found itself chewing six gobstoppers of exploding flames. Head covered in soot, it fell backwards from its perch, screaming in pain. Huge wings snapped open. The great beast flapped once, with the sound of a thunderclap, and flew away to gobble snow with its burning, ruined mouth.

In the midnight sky, five other dragons decided that tangling with wizards might not be a good idea. Instead, they screeched in rage and circled the Bleak Fortress, flaming into the sky, which – the dragons thought – looked pretty darned terrifying but meant they were at a safe distance from the dreadful men with big fiery sticks.

Dragons are evil, but they're not stupid.

Bowing, the wizards wandered up the now filthy red carpet.

A ragged cheer went up from the witches in the Great Throne Room. A spell died on Diabolica's lips as she watched her dragons retreating from the fight. "Wizards," she screeched, stamping a foot. "Who invited *wizards?*"

A screeching Esmelia was thrown through the air by a roaring demon. She landed on her back at Diabolica's feet. "No-one invited 'em," she grouched. "How did they get through the snow? That's what I want to know."

Professor Dentrifice's eyes lit up as they rested on the scowling figure of Esmelia. "Oh, we walked," he said cheerfully. "Mysterious pathways and shadowy tracks, don't you know? Thought we might offer some assistance."

"You means you that all that time I was stuck at the Goblin's Elbow, you could've walked me here?"

"But if I'd done *that* we wouldn't have had time to get to know each other my dearest Esmelia."

"Well you can just get lost again. We're just *fine* thankyousoverymuch… *waaah,*" replied Esmelia as she was dragged by the ankles back into the fight.

Around the crumbling Great Throne Room, the battle surged on. Assorted creatures of the night were finding out just how dangerous old women can be. Sam put a hand on the shaking floor and lifted herself painfully to her knees, her face still burning from the heat of the wizard's fireballs. As she watched, a spell zipped across the room. A wraith disappeared, turned into a small straw donkey. A particularly old witch, so hunched and bent it looked like she was sniffing her way along the floor, caught a demon by its horn and started banging its head on the ground, "And don't let me catch you stealing biscuits again young man," she screeched. Esmelia had her legs wrapped round a werewolf's neck. "What big hands I've got," she yelled. "All the better to pull yer ears off with." Here and there, Helza and her helpers darted through the crowd, forcing potion into the mouths of dribbling zombies. More and more choked and spluttered and turned to cast spells at the creatures they had been fighting alongside moments before.

Even so, the witches were outnumbered ten to one. Slowly, they were being pushed back while zombie-witches, ghouls, wraiths, demons, wolves, and icky things still poured through the mangled doorway of the Great Throne Room. Anyone could see that the battle was already lost.

Diabolica turned back to her dazed daughter, pointing The Black Wand of Ohh Please Don't Turn Me

Into Aaaarghh… Ribbett at her once more. "Did you really think that bunch of old ratbags could beat my army?" she hissed.

Sam didn't reply. She had a chance. As usual Diabolica was busy gabbling when she should have been fighting. Forcing herself to move, Sam lifted The White Wand of… Oi You Could Have Someone's Eye Out With That and shouted the first spell that came into her head.

Diabolica dodged to one side, but not quickly enough. Sam's magic wrapped around her, throwing her off her heels and onto her back. She screamed in pain as a sea of magically created white snakes snapped at her.

She was helpless.

Aching, Sam stood and walked forward until she was standing over her mother. "This isn't about my army beating your army," she said wearily. "It's not even about *me* beating *you*. It's about not allowing you turn everything to darkness. *Please* stop this. I don't believe you're completely evil mother. There must be some goodness left in you. We can still put everything right. There's no need to fight if you'll just *stop.*"

Diabolica stopped thrashing against the snakes and looked up at her daughter, tears springing into her eyes. "Maybe you're right," she whispered. "I've allowed the black magic to take me over. Perhaps it's because I never knew my own mother. Perhaps if I just allowed myself to love you I could find a way back again."

Diabolica winced as the snakes pulled tight around her, tears rolling down her cheeks. "Ah, this is a *nasty* spell." She breathed. "Don't make the same mistakes as me Samantha. Don't let the darkness take you."

"Just tell me you'll stop and I'll end it," Sam whispered.

"Yes," Diabolica said quietly. "Maybe there is still a chance for me. I-I'm sorry darling." Her face twisted in pain as the coiled snakes hissed. She shivered. Closing her eyes, the Wicked But Beautiful Witch Queen of All the World whispered, "I'm slipping away…"

Tears pouring down her face, Sam waved The White Wand of… Oi You Could Have Someone's Eye Out With That. The snakes disappeared. Holding her hand out, she said, "Give it to me. Give me The Black Wand of Ohh Please Don't Turn Me Into Aaaarghh… Ribbett."

Her head drooping, Diabolica staggered to her feet and lifted the wand. Sam reached for it, just as her mother snatched it back. "I always said you ghastly goody-goody types are rubbish at lying," she snickered. "Take note dear. *That's* how it's done." The Black Wand of Ohh Please Don't Turn Me Into Aaaarghh… Ribbett flared with power once again. Diabolica put her fingers down her throat and pretended to be sick. "I can't believe I had to say all that stuff," she gagged. "Maybe I can find my way back with *luuuurve.* Ugh. Re-*volting.*"

Sam stepped back. "Deadly Nightshade," she whispered sadly, pointing The White Wand of… Oi You Could Have Someone's Eye Out With That. "You really are a *terrible* mother. If you win, the entire universe will eventually freeze over you know. I read that."

Diabolica shrugged. "Ooops," she said.

Once again, the mighty wands met in battle. The Great Throne Room blazed with light and darkness as magic blossomed between Diabolica and Sam. For the first time, Sam tasted fear in her mouth, and cursed herself for letting Diabolica go free.

Ringo, where are you?

At the end of the hall a tiny speck bobbed crazily through the air past burning pointy hats and thrashing fists and swinging frying pans.

Yes.

A new spell, crackling evil ripped towards her. Sam tore her eyes away from her familiar and countered it. This time a crack opened beneath her feet. The magic of the two wands was tearing the mountain to pieces.

"I can do this forever, you know," Diabolica yelled. "Until your pathetic little army is crushed. And then *you*. Sooner or later, I *am* going to win."

Outside the wrecked windows a crooked turret collapsed, throwing up clouds of snow and crushed stone with a roar that could hardly be heard over the fighting.

Sam didn't answer but glanced down at her precious wand. Deep inside, she had always known that it would end like this, battling with her mother, the two of them tearing the world apart with the power of The White Wand of... Oi You Could Have Someone's Eye Out With That and The Black Wand of Ohh Please Don't Turn Me Into Aaaarghh... Ribbett. The fight would never stop until one of them was dead.

Deep inside, she had always known... And so, she had prepared one last nasty surprise for Diabolica.

Slashing her wand to counter spell after spell that Diabolica was hurling at her, Sam held up her hand, palm open, as Ringo dived towards her and dropped a small, crumpled ancient papyrus.

Sam's fingers closed around it.

23

The Witch is Back

It was easy to keep magic pouring from The White Wand of... Oi You Could Have Someone's Eye Out With That. Her wand seemed to know what to do. Holding it high, Sam let it flow. She wasn't trying to beat Diabolica now, just keep her busy. A spray of white twinkles jetted between them. Again, the ground rocked as it met the dark fire of The Black Wand of Ohh Please Don't Turn Me Into Aaaarghh... Ribbett. With a jolt that shook the Bleak Fortress, the crack in the floor opened wider. A demon screamed and clutched at air as it fell headlong into the pit that had opened up.

Glancing around the Throne Room, Sam saw wizards cracking skulls with their staffs; witches giving creatures the evil eye and then, because it was much more painful than the evil eye, putting the boot in. Esmelia was fighting furiously but edging towards Diabolica. Sam almost smiled to herself. The old witch never gave up. Even with the earth splitting beneath her feet and the Bleak Fortress falling around her, she was still trying to grab The Black Wand of Ohh Please Don't Turn Me Into Aaaarghh… Ribbett and become Most Superior High and Wicked Witch.

Sam's eyes moved on. Dot and Enid were playing frying pan tennis with a ghoul's head, Blanche Nightly was at the centre of a swirl of ghosts who were throwing chunks of fallen ceiling at cringing werewolves. Helza was sitting on the back of a whirling zombie witch, forcing potion between her lips.

And still the creatures of the night were forcing them back.

Sam gritted her teeth. With one sweep of The White Wand of… Oi You Could Have Someone's Eye Out With That, she could defeat Diabolica's army, but she couldn't drop her guard for a second.

Neither could Diabolica.

They were locked together in combat until the bitter end.

So, thought Sam. *It's time to make an ending.*

Closing her eyes, Sam reached out with her mind. *Balance. It's all about balance.*

She felt it. The magic of the universe. For a brief moment she touched it but, as always, it slipped from her grasp; too enormous for any witch – no matter how powerful – to hold. Forcing herself to relax, Sam tried again. It was like trying to pick up an elephant with a pair of tweezers, but for a second her eyes glowed golden.

Crown tipping forward over one eye, the Wicked but Lovely Witch Queen of All the World threw fresh magic at Sam. The White Wand of… Oi You Could Have Someone's Eye Out With That responded.

Balance.

The wand didn't matter. In a flash of understanding Sam saw it for what it truly was. Just a piece of old bone that had sucked away a tiny, tiny bit of the universe's magic. Suddenly, she couldn't remember why she had been so desperate to save it. The magic should be free, she realised, not trapped.

Suddenly, everything was *clear.*

The wand hadn't turned white because she was good but because it balanced The Black Wand of Ohh Please Don't Turn Me Into Aaaarghh… Ribbett. Light and dark, good and bad, chaos and order: the universe demanded balance.

The universe *was* balance and she was part of the universe. Not completely good, and not completely evil. Like most people – even Esmelia – a little bit of both.

This time when Sam reached out for magic she found that she could hold it easily. Space and time spun around her. She could control it all.

It was *really* cool.

Eyes glowing the colour of suns, Sam's feet left the floor. She dropped the papyrus that Ringo had brought. She didn't need a scrap of old paper.

"W-what are you doing?" gasped Diabolica slashing with The Black Wand of Ohh Please Don't Turn Me Into Aaaarghh… Ribbett. In a blaze of purple, an agony spell hissed across the Great Throne Room.

Letting The White Wand of… Oi You Could Have Someone's Eye Out With That wand fall to her side, Sam smiled gently and held out her free hand. The purple lights faded. The spell vanished.

Her jaw sagging, Diabolica took a step backwards. *It is time.*

Raising The White Wand of… Oi You Could Have Someone's Eye Out With That Sam spoke a single word. In her hands the carved bone stopped glittering and crumbled to dust.

"NO!" screamed Diabolica. Her jaw sagged as The Black Wand of Ohh Please Don't Turn Me Into Aaaarghh… Ribbett, too, fell away to nothing in her

hand. "You *idiot!* You complete and utter *cretin!* What have you done?"

Around Sam the energies of a thousand suns swirled in a blaze of colour. She smiled and stretched out her hands, shivering with tingly pleasure as magic raced through her and out into the world. Diabolica's black magic was swept away like leaves in a hurricane.

"You twazzock. You stupid great biscuit-headed spanner!" Diabolica was beside herself with rage, jumping up and down and pulling out clumps of her own hair.

"Nooooo," screeched Esmelia, pulling the brim of her hat over her ears. "What have you done to me wand you little maggot."

From above, Sam grinned at them. She was enjoying herself immensely. Having the whole of space and time to command was waaaay more fun than having a silly little wand. "Now *that's* magic," she laughed.

The Earth shuddered with relief. Winter was over. The Midwinter Moon had passed. Somewhere deep in the magic, Sam tasted Spring in the air, the hint of flowers getting ready to push themselves, yawning, through the ground; the promise of a warm breezes and bright days ahead. The slightest tang of strawberries.

The spells of The Black Wand of Ohh Please Don't Turn Me Into Aaaarghh… Ribbett were broken. The zombie-witches that Helza hadn't already potioned suddenly blinked, their minds clear.

Frogs throughout the Bleak Fortress became human beings once more.

"You fool," hissed Diabolica. "You've ruined *everything*. I'll get you for this."

"Oh, I don't sink so," said a voice behind her.

Diabolica whirled. Standing tall at the head of a thousand witches was a tall woman with glowing red eyes, wicked looking fangs and a hairdo like a large, shapely, bum. A werewolf sat, panting, at her feet. She patted it. Around the hall, ghouls and demons backed away, bowing to the Most Superior High and Wicked Witch.

Cakula von Drakula had returned to the Bleak Fortress.

The witch was back.

Magic faded from Sam's eyes. Drifting gently downwards, she felt her feet rest on the floor once more.

Diabolica backed away from Cakula, her eyes fixed on the vampire-witch. Sam watched as she pushed her crown straight with one hand; the other was already twitching as Diabolica began summoning magic. It was

just the normal everyday kind of magic but, Sam reminded herself, Diabolica was still a powerful sorceress.

Not as powerful as Cakula though.

The Most Superior High and Wicked Witch raised her own hands, magic sparkling at the tips off her fingers.

"So Diabolica Nightshade," Cakula said in a voice that carried all the centuries she had been, sort of, alive. "Now you vant to fight me, huh?"

"No, she doesn't," said Sam, stepping forward to stand between Cakula and her mother.

Cakula raised an eyebrow. She looked around herself at the ruins of the Bleak Fortress. Trampled and burned pointy hats were scattered everywhere. The earth still groaned and shifted. A ghoul drifted forward, "ssssuffering!" it hissed. "There iss no ssuffering here. We wisssh to return to the dark pits of horridnessss."

"Vun moment Barry," said Cakula, glancing at the ghoul. Holding up a finger she looked back at Sam. "You wish to protect Diabolica Nightshade, younk lady?"

"She's my mother," Sam replied. "And now it's over," Sam said firmly.

"Do you have to be so *good* all the time?" sighed Diabolica. "It really is very dull Samantha."

"Ummm… do you ever keep quiet?" Sam replied.

"And, by the way, it's *Sam*. Samantha sounds like a horse coughing."

Diabolica shrugged. "Whatever you like dear." Giving Cakula a wink, she continued. "My daughter says no more suffering. Sorry about that. While you argue about it I'll just get my coat and be on my way. Cheerio." Spotting a witch in the crowd, she shouted, "Come along Mandy, let's be off."

The badly dressed reporter and former henchperson, Mandy Snoutley, delved into a pocket for a pencil and a notepad, talking aloud as she scribbled a story for *The Cackler*. "Amid scenes of celebration," she said, "complete and utter failure of a witch queen Deadly Nightshade was beaten in a magical duel by a small child."

"You just cannot get decent henchpeople these days," muttered Diabolica, turning away.

Sam caught her by the arm, "Just a moment," she said. "Mother, do you really think I'm stupid enough to let you just wander off to start plotting again?"

"Oh, I *promise* I'll be good from now on," Diabolica replied with a wave of her hand. "I've learned my lesson, by golly. You won't catch me hatching a wicked plot to take over the world again. Now that the darkness has gone I can see what a terrible mistake I made. Oh no. I'm a changed character me."

Sam rolled her eyes.

"If you insist, I vill not hurt her," replied Cakula interrupted. "But she must go somevhere safe."

"Where?"

Cakula reached out. Muttering under her breath she made a complicated gesture in the air. A great tear appeared. The Most Superior High and Wicked Witch looked around at the creatures of the night. "You vill go home," she said loudly. Looking at Sam she added, "And I, too, grow veary off zis world. I will go vith them, and take Diabolica Nightshade with me."

"Errr, no thanks," said Diabolica quickly. "Sam my darling girl, you won't let them drag mummy off to some ghastly netherworld will you? It would be just too awful for words. And I *love* you."

"Oh just stop it mother," Sam snapped. Turning to Cakula, she said "Very well. She will go with you."

Cakula bowed. "I vill not return," she said. "Vill you be ze new Most Zuperior High and Vicked Vitch? You haff earned it."

"Oi," screeched Esmelia, elbowing her way through the crowd. *"I'm* Most Superior High and Wicked Witch.

It said so in *The Cackler.*"

Cakula kept her eyes on Sam. "Vell?" she said softly.

Sam thought about it. Cakula was right, she did deserve it. Once again, Penny Dreadful's words came back to her. She could be queen of all the world. Not like Diabolica though. A *good* queen. She could remake the Bleak Fortress. It would be magnificent this time; all shining towers and graceful pointy turrets. And she could make the world a better place.

Or I could just let the world be what it wants to be.

Shaking her head, Sam glanced up at Esmelia with a twinkle in her eye and said, "Esmelia's right. She is the *proper* Most Superior High and Wicked Witch."

"Yes!" screeched Esmelia jumping up and down on the broken floor of the Bleak Fortress. "At last. I'm the big stinky cheese. The head honcho. I'm the flippin' boss I am."

"Oi," yelled a witch. "No-one said anything about Stinky Sniff being Most Superior High and Wicked Witch."

Cakula glanced at her, red fire flaring in her eyes.

"But that's just fine with me," babbled the witch. "Oh yes, I always thought old Stink… errr… Esmelia would make a fine Most Superior High and Wicked

Witch, I did."

Nervously, the other witches nodded in agreement, mumbling, "Oh yes, oh yes, good old Esmelia. Three cheers and all that."

"Congratulations Esmelia," Cakula said. "Ze Bleak Fortress iz yours." She glanced around at the wreckage of the castle and, with a smile, murmured, "you might vant to redecorate."

Esmelia scowled at her.

Cakula wasn't finished though. And she hadn't forgotten that Esmelia's part in keeping her a frog for so long. "Now," she said smoothly. "As my last act as Most Superior High and Vicked Vitch, I release Sam from her apprenticeship. From this day on, she is free off you."

The old witch turned pale green. Her jaw dropped open. "You can't…" she began. But Cakula could. The law was the law and for the moment at least, Cakula von Drakula was still the Most Superior High and Wicked Witch.

"Thanks," Sam said quickly. "But I'd still like to stay with Esmelia." She looked up at the warty old witch and smiled. "So long as we can go back to the cottage. I'm sick of this place."

"Y-you're going to stay with Stinky Sniff," gasped a

voice in the crowd. Helza's purple head appeared. "Are you, like, totally bonkers?"

"No, I don't think I am," said Sam. "It's where I belong."

Tears pricked at the corners of Esmelia's eyes. She blinked. "You want to stay with *me?*" she asked with a raspy voice.

"Yup. That is if you still want the company."

The old witch pulled herself together. *I ain't crying,* she told herself firmly. *It's just dust in me eyes.* She tried a scowl. For the first time in her life couldn't quite manage it. She tried harder, and this time it came. "Well, you'll have to work harder," she scowled. "And if you gives me any cheek…"

"I know," interrupted Sam. "If I gives you any cheek it'll be head first into the oven."

The Bleak Fortress trembled again, the few bits of wall still standing crashing to the ground. "Alright then," Esmelia said roughly. "We'll have to find a new cottage though."

Sam smiled up at her. "Oh, that won't be a problem," she said.

Her eyes glowed golden.

Far, far away in a tiny clearing in Pigsnout Wood

there was a whirl of golden light. A small cottage appeared, it's roof sagging and its walls wonky. In the attic room an old bed squeaked. On a small table next to it was a stuffed badger, a skull with a candle on top and a book called *Think Yourself Witch: 100 Steps Towards Becoming a Crone.*

The power of the two wands could not turn back time, but Sam could.

Really really cool, she thought to herself.

Epilogue

"This is a good bit," said Esmelia, peering over the top of *The Cackler* from her favourite rocking chair. "Listen. Mandy Snoutley writes: 'a small army of witches led by that most excellent of crones, Esmelia Sniff, entered the Bleak Fortress by stealth, though none of the witches will now say how it was done. Inside, they surprised Diabolica and bravely fought her army…'"

Sam lifted her own head from the pages of *Think Yourself Witch*. "Does it say anything about me?" she asked.

"Only that you're a right pranny for destroying The Black Wand of Ohh Please Don't Turn Me Into Aaaarghh… Ribbett and breaking the Bleak Fortress," sniffed Esmelia. "Witches ain't happy about that."

Sam sighed and blew hair out of her eyes. It had gone a bit greasy and had one or two twigs tangled in it. She was dressed in patched black jeans and a black vest. Spring had arrived as if it was trying to make up for lost time. Outside the open windows of Esmelia's cottage brightly-coloured birds chased each other through the warm air while bunnies and squirrels and hedgehogs frolicked through the trees. Esmelia glared at them until they went away.

"Anything else?"

"The Grand High Coven are thinking about changing the laws of witchcraft. Anyone who wants to take over the world will have to have a special license. Some are saying that witches should be allowed to get married and all. Disgustin' that is. And, oooooh, here's some good news…"

"What?" said Sam excitedly. "Does Mandy say how I saved the world?"

"No, there's a jumble sale this afternoon."

Sam looked down at her book. *You should go,* Lilith Dwale scrawled across the page. *Jumble sales are what being a witch is all about. And you might pick up a decent hat.*

"I think I'll keep the one I've got for a while longer," Sam muttered. "Besides, I'm going to visit Helza this afternoon." There was a scribbling noise from above. Sam crossed her eyes and peered up at the brim of Esmelia's second-best hat. A piece of paper spilled over the edge. Holding a tiny stub of pencil between his front legs, Ringo was busy writing his book. The little beetle leaned over the brim and waved at her. Sam frowned, wondering where he had managed to find glasses and a hat small enough to fit.

Her thoughts were interrupted by a knock at the door.

"Go and get that," grouched Esmelia, shaking her newspaper and picking her nose. "It'll prob'ly be another little girl wantin' to be an apprentice. Tell her I've already got one but she's welcome to sit in the oven for six hours at gas mark four."

With a sigh, Sam got up and opened the door. Professor Sebastian Dentrifice stood on the narrow path, twiddling his fingers. Behind him, Wolfbang Pigsibling peered around the wizard's massive bulk and grinned at Sam.

She grinned back.

The professor coughed. "Ahhh," he said, blushing beneath his beard. "Is… umm… the lovely… errr… is the Most Superior High and Wickedest Witch at home."

"What does you want?" growled Esmelia, looming suddenly behind her apprentice. "Coming round her and disturbing an old lady's nose picking."

"Umm… I was just wondering… That is… could I possibly buy you dinner tonight?"

"Yes you possibly could," said Esmelia. "I'll have freshly battered slug with chips. Leave it on the doorstep and then get lost."

"Actually… I… errr… meant…could I take *you* out for dinner tonight?"

Esmelia glared a glare that could have dropped a charging rhinoceros. "Go out to dinner with a wizard?" she screeched. "I wouldn't be seen dead with a beardy nincompoop like you. I'd rather eat me own earwax than go to a *very fancy and expensive restaurant* with a squid-brained walrus in curly shoes."

"Shall we say seven then?"

As Esmelia drew her breath to screech again, Sam nudged her.

"Alrightseveno'clock," Esmelia gabbled. From somewhere beneath her ragged skirt came a croaking noise.

"A-ha," said Professor Dentrifice. "You've got frogs in your underwear again."

"No I ain't," snapped Esmelia, slamming the door.

Sam smiled. Esmelia was going out on a date. Which meant she'd need something to wear. Plus, deep down in her witchy soul she was feeling the call of the jumble sale. Lilith was right, she realised, jumble sales were what being a witch was all about. She'd be late for Helza but being late was also what being a witch was all about.

She whistled for her broom.

With Esmelia sitting behind, holding her hat with one hand while her other gripped Sam's waist, the two witches crashed through branches heavy with buds.

"Esmelia?" said Sam over her shoulder.

"What?" grumped the old witch.

"There's one thing I don't understand."

"Bah, there's loads of things *you* don't understand."

Sam ignored her. "If you knew I wasn't really evil when you arrived at the Bleak Fortress, why did you slap me?"

There was silence as Esmelia thought about it. Eventually, she said, "I likes to keep in practice dearie."

With a sigh, Sam pointed the broom into the clear sky and felt it lurch forward with a burst of speed. Some things, she thought to herself, would never change.

And, on the whole, she was really quite glad about that.

With love to Maia, Buffy and Sam: my beautiful children.

Martin Howard

Also Available

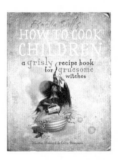

Witches at War!
The Wickedest Witch
(Book 1)

Available as:
Hardback:
9781843651314

Ebook:
9781843652168

Witches at War!
The White Wand
(Book 2)

Available as:
Hardback:
9781843651345

Ebook:
9781843652182

How to Cook Children

Available as:
Paperback:
9781843651796